SANDPIPER

Rhys Lloyd

For my family, those who are here now, those who have gone and those yet to arrive.

11 June 2015

Introduction

My youngest brother, who is a doctor, although not mine, once told me that one way to deal with life was to write down how you feel. I am not sure whether his suggestion was based on a view that if something goes from your mind to the page then you won't worry so much; or so that one could see how mad it all sounded when written down; or if he was just trying to get rid of me. Anyway, following his advice, I started writing it down. I do think it helped. But it felt like I only wrote down the bad stuff. So, I turned my mind to how to write in a balanced but realistic and true way about life and what it means and what it's all about.

Like many young people who came of age in the late seventies, I was into bands like Joy Division and wanted to write poetry like the lyrics of their lead singer Ian Curtis (who hung himself, perfect moody fodder). I still have my poetry from that period – stuff I wrote between 1978 and 1983. Like all rather poor teenage and post teenage angst, it features a little bit of politics (left wing of course), some stuff directed at the girl of the moment, and, on reflection, an unhealthy obsession with death and dying. There is also lots of stuff about, or set by, the sea. I grew up on the coast and, when I am not thinking about death, I think about the beach and the sea and, by implication I guess, my childhood.

I grew up on the coast of south Wales, the eldest of three sons. I went to the local state school, was academically inclined, did well, went to university and then came to London to work. I joined a large firm in 1983 and was still there thirty plus years later, living in North London with my wife and children, when I started to write this.

If you asked my friends and family, they would say I always worried about stuff and no doubt if you delved into my childhood it would all stem from that time I was locked in a cupboard with a dead uncle. The cupboard must have been on the edge of a cliff - because I am also scared of heights - and full of spiders, because they scare me too.

So far as I am aware, such a cupboard did not exist, nor was I locked in it but no doubt I could get enough therapy to construct a theory as to why I worry about stuff. The point is, though, that sometimes I do, and it can be pretty disabling.

In writing, I am conscious that the negatives will come out and may be shared with people for whom they became a real burden. There is a risk that people think I am trivialising things, that I have been lucky to be able to indulge these issues and that I do not recognise some of the hurt I have caused. Nothing could be further from the truth. I appreciate the support I have been given. It's part of what makes me vested in telling this story.

When I started to write, people often asked me what I was going to write about. Of course, I know what I'm trying to say; I can only hope that, as you read on, you will enjoy coming on this journey with me. Some of this stuff is based upon what I wrote before. Other parts I am writing now from fictionalised memories or an imagined future.

I have a lovely wife and three great kids. I have a proper grown-up job. But my wife gave birth to the children and brought them up. I didn't build my own business; I have worked for someone else for thirty-two years. So, all I have to leave behind is how I lived and what I thought while I was here.

Rhys Lloyd

PART ONE - BIRTH AND BOYHOOD

1961 to 1980

From the Big Bang, to the much smaller bang, which conceived me, I have no memory. I have no me.

16 September 1961

I am expelled into the world (to be precise, the Maternity Ward of Luton and Dunstable General Hospital), one of 50 boys born in the UK that hour. Son of Mum and Dad, younger brother to my big sister, I am the latest Sandpiper.

I do not remember the Cuban Missile Crisis, the Beatles, England winning the World Cup, or moving to Wales, but I am told that they all happened.

25 December 1966

Watch out Laura, I say, as I speed down the garden path towards her.

She rolls to the left, in her new roller skates, and I glide past, on my new, first ever, bike.

This is the best Christmas, ever. I have had a couple of goes on Laura's old bike before but now I have my own – my red and gold machine – I am going to call it Dragon. For now, it has stabilisers but if I keep practicing Dad says I will get the hang of it and he'll take them off.

Mum tells us both to get the hang of our presents in the garden. She says it is a safer place to practice and fall over and that we will go for a walk/cycle/roll later, before tea. Tea, I think, how will I have any room to eat ever again? I ate a huge

7

Christmas lunch, having already eaten most of my selection box while I sat on Laura's bed opening our presents. Maybe I need the stabilisers to make sure that the bike can carry my weight!

I ask Dad how Santa got my bike down the chimney – after some searching, I had found it wrapped and under the tree when I came down for breakfast. Dad says Santa had left it in the garage, not everything had to come down the chimney. I had asked Santa for a bike in the letter I sent him. We all did letters to Santa at school at the start of December.

> *"Dear Father Christmas,*
>
> *I have been a good boy this year. You can ask my Mum and Dad. I have put out the rubbish and cleaned everyone's shoes every week. I have said sorry when I have been rude, and I got a good report from Rainbow class at school.*
>
> *Can I have a bike, some sweets and some comics for Christmas this year?*
>
> *And can you bring something for Laura, and Mum and Dad.*
>
> *Thank you."*

Santa had almost not come though, because I am so excited on Christmas Eve that I can't sleep.

"Go to sleep now, or Santa won't come" says Mum.

I should go to sleep, I do want Santa to come, but I am too excited. If I just pretend to sleep will that work? I do that with Mum and Dad sometimes, but will that fool Santa?

We put out the sherry and mince pie for Santa and the bowl of water for his reindeer. Mum put the pillowcase at the end of my bed for Santa to put my presents in.

I must have fallen asleep though, because when I woke up the pillowcase was full. Laura had one too and we opened them together.

"At five in the morning!", as Laura kept reminding me

all day. After we open our pillowcases, she sends me downstairs so she can get some more sleep. She tells me not to wake Mum and Dad yet. I go quietly downstairs, but Mum is already up. She has been getting the turkey ready.

"Happy Christmas Joseph", she says, and kisses me on the cheek.

"Happy Christmas Mum", I say, and smile. "Can I open one of the presents under the tree?"

"Not yet, wait for Dad and Laura, and then we will have breakfast. Why don't you watch TV?"

I turn the TV on – it is showing a Laurel and Hardy movie. I like them, but, when Mum goes to the toilet, I take a quick look at the presents under the tree. None of them look large enough to be a bike. Santa has obviously been – the sherry and mince pie are gone – but no bike? I am going to have to look harder.

I finally spot a large parcel, hidden behind the tree – that's sneaky. It looks big enough to be a bike. Does it have my name on? Yes! I hear Mum returning from the toilet and retreat back to the sofa.

I like Laurel and Hardy. Mum says I look a bit like Stan Laurel and sometimes, to make her laugh, I scratch my head like he does.

11 August 1967

"…who wants an ice cream?" asks Dad.

"Me," I say.

"And me,"

"Catherine?"

"No thanks. Just a small one for them, I don't want this picnic to go to waste."

Do I have time to go into the sea before Dad comes back with the ice creams? I reckon so.

"Mum can I go back in the sea?"

"Only if Laura goes with you"

"I've only just got dry!" protests Laura.

"You can come with me Mum. You haven't been in the sea yet."

This is true, but I know that Mum doesn't really like going in the sea, she says it's not very clean, and messes up her hair.

Much to my surprise though, she agrees.

"Yes, OK. Watch the bags Laura."

"And watch my sandcastle," I say.

I have built an amazing sandcastle. Dad and Laura helped but it is my castle. There is a moat, a bridge, a castle keep with a seaweed flag. I would like to live somewhere like this. Not this actual one, it's too small and will get washed away by the sea later, but a real castle like this one.

We went to visit one a few months ago. It was really a bit of a ruin and would need a lot of work if I was going to live there but, other than that, it would have been a great place. Dad and I would patrol the ramparts at night and learn how to sword fight during the day.

Next to the castle were some stepping stones that went across a river. The castle would be easy to defend if enemy soldiers attacked from that side. We could build a lever system where the stones moved up when the enemy stood on them, tipping them into the river.

Even though no one had put the lever systems in yet, I slipped off one of the stones halfway across. Since the river was two feet deep, it was not a big problem, but it did shorten the visit as we had not brought any spare clothes with us.

Now, though, I am supposed to get wet. I race Mum into the sea.

The water is freezing, even though it is August. But that won't stop me. I throw myself headfirst into an oncoming

10

wave. Not a great idea, as I swallow mouthfuls of seawater. Mum pulls me to the surface.

"Careful!" she says, "You don't want to drown before your ice cream!"

I don't want to drown after my ice cream either. I throw myself at the next wave.

Laura had told me - so it must be true – that there is a ship that sank somewhere near here nearly a hundred years ago and the wreck is still there, at the bottom of the sea. There is no lighthouse here, in Caswell Bay, which is maybe why the ship sank, because it didn't see the rocks.

The nearest lighthouse to here is on Mumbles Head. We have been to visit it. Maybe if I can't live in a castle I can live in a lighthouse and save ships from drowning.

When it's night-time, we can see the light from the Mumbles Head lighthouse from our caravan up above the Bay. The lighthouse light is really bright when the moon isn't there.

Why isn't the moon there sometimes? Laura told me that it was the moon that made the waves but there are waves all the time, even when the moon's not there. I don't really understand the waves either – they will come in later and swallow up my amazing sandcastle, but then they will go out again. Where do they go? To another beach, to wash someone else's sandcastle away?

We have been to this beach and stayed in this caravan park on holiday before although it usually rains. Today, though, it is really sunny and warm enough to even go in the sea.

I surface. Mum is standing ankle deep in the shallows, waving at someone. At Dad, who is obviously back with the ice cream. I better go and get it before it melts. Not before I've buried my feet though. On my way out of the sea I stand at the edge of the incoming waves and watch my feet gradually sink into the sand. Further and further as each wave washes over them. Even without a melting ice cream to go and eat, I never stay there long enough to see whether I would sink all the way down, although I wonder what would happen if I did.

"Race you back to Dad", I shout and set off. I win. I eat my ice cream and Mum gives me some squash to drink.

***

"Come on then Laura, Joseph, let's go fishing!' says Dad. We have brought our nets with us and we always hope that Dad will take us to the rock pools to fish. There aren't really any fish in the rock pools – so it isn't really "fishing" – but there are crabs and shrimps as well as living seashells. You can't catch the seashells as they are always stuck to the rocks.

I got a sea life I–Spy book for Christmas and I am still trying to find all the creatures that are in it. I have got lots already. But, so far, no starfish, nor sea cucumber. Last time we were here, Dad threw a piece of cucumber from our sandwiches in a rock pool and claimed it. Funny, but it didn't count.

Laura brings two buckets with her and we fill them with water, and a few pebbles and seaweed, ready for our catch. Dad had made the nets from his garden equipment - a bamboo pole with some strawberry netting attached. They are the same nets we use for catching butterflies. That is harder than crabs and shrimps because they can fly out of reach. Although they pretty soon come back to the flowers in the garden and you can try again.

Today, though, it is rock pools, not flower beds. Catching a crab is more exciting than a few shrimps, but harder as they move faster and hide better. The other way to catch crabs is to find them buried in the sand after the tide has gone out, but at the moment it is on its way in.

"Dad, I'm going to catch a crab, and let it live in my sandcastle"

"Until the tide comes in" says Dad. He laughs, grabs

12

me round the shoulders and picks me up…

***

"…out, you are out."

"No, it hit the bat, not my leg," says Laura.

"Give her one more chance, Joseph," says Dad.

I put my crab – Dad caught it, but gave it to me – in my sandcastle, so that we can play French Cricket. I don't know why it is called "French" cricket. Do the French not have much space for a proper cricket pitch? I am also not sure of the rules. When we play it at school, you aren't allowed to move your feet if you are in, you just have stay facing in one direction and defend your legs with the bat. People are also allowed to bowl as hard as they like.

When my family play, though, you are allowed to move round to face the bowler each time and no one is allowed to throw the ball hard. It is easier to stay in, which is great if you are batting but frustrating if it isn't your turn.

I manage twenty-five runs on my turn – one run each time I hit the ball further away than the bowler - before being caught by Mum. Now it is Laura's turn; she only has five runs but she is still in. I think I bowled her out but Dad, the umpire, says not.

Mum and Dad are never in for long, they are always making a mistake and hitting the ball in the air where we can catch it. Or Mum will miss the ball completely sometimes.

Laura hits the next one up in the air towards me.

"Catch it!" Mum and Dad shout. I keep watching the ball and run to where I think it will land. That looks like it will be in the sea, but that is not going to stop me, she's been in long enough.

Wading in, daps and all, I catch it and fall over – in that order so I think I caught it first. I get up, and proudly hold the ball above my head. "Howzat?!" I cry.

"Out!" says dad.

"Good catch!" says Laura.

"One more inning for that," says Mum

Maybe if I can't be a soldier or a lighthouse keeper, I can play cricket when I grow up, even if I have to play it in France.

15 May 1968

"Hey kid, why don't you come and play with us?"

"I can't, I'm not allowed to leave the garden."

"How old are you?"

"I'm six."

"And you're not allowed to leave the garden?"

"No. My mum is out, and she told me I could go in our garden but nowhere else. She's locked the house."

"So, she won't know if you come and play with us."

"No, I'm fine."

"Your loss, mate."

He turns to his friends, "What a baby!"

They cross into the fields opposite our house.

Later on, loads of houses will be built between our house and the beach but when we first moved in there was nothing between our estate and the sea, about a mile away, except a couple of scrubby fields.

I do not see the boys for ages. I am content catching, or trying to catch, butterflies. My father has lots of boxes in the garage full of dead butterflies and moths, which he collected when he was a child, all neatly pinned and labelled. I have so far failed to replicate it. Even when I catch one, I am not sure how, or whether to kill it. I have this theory that if you kill something, its much bigger parents will come and get you later. Who needs a cabbage white the size of car snatching me up in

14

its jaws? Jaws: do butterflies have jaws? Or they have that long proboscis thing for drinking nectar, it could drain me of blood. Mum would come home to a lifeless whitened corpse.

I am having more luck replicating Dad's stamp collection. A fire engine rumbles past the house. I have never seen one in real life before. I see why it is here now, there is smoke coming from the fields. Wow, that is exciting, unless it is heading this way. It will be OK now though as the firemen are here. And it is, soon.

One of the firemen comes back down the road to our gate.

"Hey, can I have word?"

"What's your name?"

"Did you see anyone around who might have lit the fire?"

"No."

"Those boys said you did it," he says, gesturing up the road to the group who had passed by earlier.

"They said they saw you playing with matches in your garden and then go over there."

"I'm not allowed to leave the garden."

"Where are your parents?"

"Out."

"When will they be back?"

"I don't know."

"Did you have anything to do with the fire?"

"No, really, I am not allowed to leave the garden."

"And you didn't?"

"I didn't."

"Well, someone lit it. We'll come back and see your parents later."

"OK."

"Tell them they can ring when they get back. Here's the number."

15

Mum believes me when I tell her and tells the firemen as much. I hear her shouting down the phone.

"You really think he would have left the garden when I told him not to?"

"What about the other boys, where are they from? Are you going to speak to their parents?"

It pays to have an alibi, and a healthy fear of your mum, as I did really want to go with the boys.

22 October 1969

"Have you brushed your teeth?" asks Dad.

"Yes. Mum saw me do it."

"OK, get into bed."

"Will you read me a story?"

"Yes, you get into bed, and I'll be back in a minute to read to you."

Dad doesn't read to me every night, sometimes it is Mum and sometimes neither of them. Laura used to read to me when I was younger, but she is, according to Dad, going through her 'angry teenager' phase where she pretends that she doesn't have a family. I am not sure why she would want to pretend that. One of the boys at my school, Ian, has no family. His parents were killed in a car crash and he lives with his 'aunt and uncle'. They are much older than Mum and Dad and Ian always seems sad.

I can read myself now, but it isn't the same, it feels like homework and I never feel like I am in the story. It's just looking at the words on the page. When Dad reads, it is like being in the world of the story. He is reading me Rosemary Sutcliff at the moment, a story where a Roman boy is trying find his long-lost friend who had the other half of a golden coin. I even have half a coin (not gold, just a copper penny) on my bedside table.

16

I love history stories, "the olden days" as my parents call them, before even they were born. Kings and queens, knights in shining armour, bravery and battles – it is all incredibly exciting. I spend many hours setting out my toy soldiers in intricate battlefields or besieging my fort.

If I am going to be a soldier – I am considering it, or a fireman – then I would prefer the old days and the big marches and battles. Nowadays it is all planes and missiles and bombs and stuff, apparently.

Laura told me that there was nearly a war when she was ten when the Americans and Russians had threatened to fire missiles at each other until there were no people left, even in Wales. But they had made up and it is OK now. That's good.

I still haven't got into bed. If dad gets back before I do then there will be no story!

I find the Rosemary Sutcliff book, and clamber into my bed. I wait for Dad. I can hear his voice downstairs. It is raised, along with Mum's. I cannot make out much of what they are saying, but I hear some of it.

"Stop trying to be the nice parent."

"Staying out too late."

"She is going to waste her life! "

It sounds like another row about Laura and her behaviour. At some point Laura has obviously come home as her voice joins in.

"Everyone else does."

"I don't want to go to university."

"Your Dad agrees with me," says Mum.

Followed by stomping and Laura's bedroom door slamming.

I put the Sutcliff down and turn out my light. No story tonight.

1 August 1970

Another Summer. No school. Spending it with my two best friends, Andy Pritchard and William Shepherd.

Before it happened, we had had great times, always going down to the beach.

Our favourite place; playing in the waves; climbing the rocks; fishing for crabs; building amazing sandcastles. We were there almost every day during the holidays.

When the tide was out there was plenty of sand for a football game or to ride your bike. When it was in then you could climb on the rocks and skim pebbles on the sea.

William lives nearest the beach, so we usually go to his house on the way. Mum knows his mum, so she is happy for me to go round to his house and to the beach. So long as we are back before it gets dark.

It was during the summer holidays. Today, we meet at William's house at about ten in the morning.

William's mum introduced him.

"Hello, Joe, this is Will's cousin Peter, he is staying with us for the week."

"Will is going to take him to the beach with you three."

Peter is younger than me, maybe seven. He looks cheerful but a little bit weedy. He is from Birmingham and has no brothers or sisters. William has a brother, but he is fourteen and far too cool to hang out with us, unless Laura is on the scene too.

Andy arrives, late as usual, for which I have to give him a dead leg. William's mum gives us some crisps and drinks to take to the beach. I put mine in my bag with my towel and trunks. I see that Mum has also put some sunscreen in my bag. Andy says that only softies wear sunscreen, so I don't put any on.

There are two ways to the beach from William's house

– the path that runs down the side of the golf course, or the "Tunnel". The Tunnel is quicker but much harder as you have to slide down on your bum. It's quite steep, and you also have to try and avoid being stabbed by the gorse bushes. Someone must have dug out the mud above the sea wall, but that will have been a while ago, because the Tunnel has been there as long as I can remember. It gets a bit overgrown in the winter but by now it has been used by hundreds of us and is, while difficult, clear enough to use. Also, it comes out directly onto the best climbing rocks at the beach. Andy had been the first of the three of to use the Tunnel, two summers ago, and we had been down it maybe a dozen times since.

"Are we going to use it?" I ask William.

"Yeah, sure."

"Is Peter old enough?"

"Yeah, sure."

We climb over the fence out of the back of William's garden and cross the road. Peter follows.

"Race you" I shout and set off, too fast it turns out, as Andy catches and overtakes me long before we reach the entrance.

You aren't supposed to use it. It starts behind a wall and there is a sign telling us it is private land and "Trespassers will be prosecuted." I am never sure what the land could be privately used for though, it is just a patch covered in ferns and gorse that fall steeply from the fence onto the rocks below. Maybe the owner wants to just use the Tunnel himself. If I owned the land, I would charge people to use it, and at least make some money from owning it that way.

William and Peter arrive at the wall and we clamber over. I have to help Peter get down on the other side.

"Where are we going," he asks.

"Down to the beach, this way."

"How do we get down this way?"

"There's a tunnel over there that goes down."

"Is it safe?"

"Yes, of course."

"Auntie Lucy told William to look after me."

So, William's mum is called Lucy, that's quite a nice name. My mum is called Catherine. That is a nice name too, better than my Dad's. He is called Owen, which is more of a second name, I think.

I catch up with William.

"Peter says your mum told you to look after him. I don't think he wants to go down the Tunnel."

"Tough, I'm not a babysitter!"

We arrive at the top. "Who wants to go first?" asks William. "I will," says Andy. I don't usually go first when it is the three of us. I want someone else to be the first and then it is usually me second as I don't want to be left behind at the top on my own. Andy puts his bag down – we will throw them down when somebody is at the bottom – and, crying, "Yahoo," sets off down the Tunnel.

I hear the occasional whelp of pain as he stabs himself on the gorse and then he emerges slowly onto the rocks at the bottom and waves.

"See," says William to Peter, "it's as easy as that."

"I don't want to go. I'll get hurt."

"No, you won't. Don't be a baby."

Although he is my friend, William has definitely accused me of being a baby before. There is not usually any point in arguing with him.

"Peter do you want to go next? Andy can catch you at the bottom."

"No, I don't want to go at all."

"Well, why don't I go down," I suggest, "and then there will be two of us at the bottom to catch you."

"He doesn't need anyone to catch him," mutters

William, "if he doesn't just go, I'll push him down!"

Afterwards, I wonder whether I should have said something, Peter was definitely scared, but, instead, I put my rucksack down and set myself off. It isn't too bad, because it is dry and has been well used so you can pick some speed but, as long as you keep your feet down, not too much.

"Hey," says Andy as I arrive. I get up and call out "Come on down Peter, we'll catch you."

I hear William shouting at Peter. I'd have come down quickly if he had shouted at me like that.

William shouts again, "Peter". Then nothing. And then, much more quietly, we hear a scream, a screech (that turns out to be a car using its brakes) and a loud bang on the road above.

"William, what was that?" There is no answer. We call out several times and hear nothing, so we have to come back up. You can't get back up the Tunnel (we have tried several times) so we run back round past the golf course.

It only takes us maybe ten minutes but by the time we arrive there is already an ambulance. A black car, its front and side crumpled in, is stuck on the wall. William is sat on the other side of the road with a woman talking to him, and, in the middle of the road, is Peter, with two ambulance men giving him oxygen and stuff.

William told the police later that Peter had turned and run from the top of the Tunnel, climbed over the wall and jumped off, into the path of the car. The driver said the same thing. That was how it was reported in the papers.

I tell the police that Peter didn't want to go down the Tunnel but that he didn't seem too scared. I don't mention William threatening to push him or telling him he was being a baby.

Mum and Dad and Laura come to the police station. Mum speaks to Lucy and then we leave. Andy is still there waiting for his parents.

21

I saw William again at the funeral but then he changed schools. I still see Andy, but we are not friends any more.

I never went down the Tunnel again.

18 October 1970

"Joseph," Mum shouts.

"Come on, your sister's downstairs having breakfast already. We're going to be late."

My sister, on her good days, gets me into trouble, by being well behaved and prompt and lots of other things that I am not. Now Mum says we are going to be late for school because of me. It isn't my fault anyway; I can't find my football boots. We have a match today at school and you're not allowed to play unless you bring all your kit. I have actually already been downstairs to look for them, long before Laura, but they weren't in the hall.

I like playing football. I am not very good, but I am very keen and try hard so that usually gets me in the team. No one wants to be in goal or defence, so when Mr. Jones isn't around to coach us, the game ends up with twenty of us racing across the pitch to wherever the ball is. Sometimes the swarm becomes twenty-two, when the goalies declare themselves as "rush".

So where are my boots? They aren't in my wardrobe. They aren't under my bed. They aren't on my feet – you never know! Mum once found her glasses on her head after she had looked for them for twenty minutes, and blamed me and Dad, not Laura, for hiding or losing them. She didn't apologise either, but that was Mum. For her, "sorry" was just a sign of weakness, and the important thing was that we never did it again. But they were her glasses, and they were on her head!

"Mum, I can't find my football boots."

"I put them in your kit bag last night. Now come

downstairs. We need to leave in five minutes."

How am I supposed to know that she has done that? I can never tell with my Mum. Sometimes she is helpful and does stuff like that. Sometimes it is all my responsibility and, no, she is not going to help me look. And, no, Dad isn't going to either. He usually does though. So long as Mum doesn't catch him. He isn't here this morning; he is away all week. At a conference, whatever that is, somewhere. So, he won't be coming to watch me play football today.

I run downstairs. I know Mum will leave without me if I am not ready. She has done it before. One time I tried to stop her by lying on the drive behind the car. I think she would have stopped but as she revved it and started to reverse, I lost my nerve. I was late for school that day.

Laura is sat at the kitchen table eating a slice of toast. I will have to eat mine on the run, if Mum has made me any. I see one piece on the side and grab it.

"Thanks for putting my boots in my bag." Mum says.

Why is she thanking me? I get it. "Yes, thanks Mum," I say and retreat to the bottom of the stairs to put my shoes on, slice of toast in hand.

How can I tie my shoelaces and not put the buttered toast down on the carpet? I place the toast between my teeth and deliver some high quality bows on my shoes. I learnt to tie shoelaces ages ago. Some of my friends still can't and come to school in slip-ons.

These are new shoes, so I am still trying to look after them. They aren't the best shoes I have ever seen but they are the best I have ever had myself. A rich brown, with cool patches. And a sole that makes strong circular patterns in the sand.

We bought them at the weekend, at the shoe shop. Laura had got some new shoes too. If I have to go shopping, it is better if Laura comes too as that way I play a far less

23

significant role in the whole shopping thing. Choosing my new shoes had taken about ten minutes: for Laura's it feels like it had taken at least an hour.

I don't like going shopping. I don't like shops really. Shopping for clothes is the worst. When I have to try all sorts of things on. At least my Mum comes into the changing rooms with me. I see some kids where their mum makes them come out of the cubicle and parade in front of the whole shop. That must be awful. Being in the spotlight.

Like your own birthday party, when you are the centre of attention and everyone is supposed to make a fuss of you and the clown makes you a special balloon animal. I hate that. I like birthdays, because I want to get older, and I sometimes get a good present, but the party bit is not for me.

Laura likes them, her parties, and mine. She gets to dress up. And sing and dance. She loves singing. To be fair she can actually sing quite well. She also plays the piano and the violin. I have been to see her in loads of concerts. She's really good. All of those people applauding her. That's the spotlight! I am glad I don't have to do it.

"Joseph," shouts Mum, "take that toast out of your mouth and get a plate!"

Then, just as I start to obey, "No, we haven't got time. Go and eat it over the sink and get in the car."

I return to the kitchen. Laura smiles at me. She hands me a plate and pushes a chair out for me to sit at the kitchen table, then gets up and goes to speak to Mum.

"Thanks," I mutter and sit to eat my toast.

Our tea for that evening is on the kitchen table already - tinned steak and kidney pie and some potatoes, which I will be peeling after school. There are only three potatoes, I guess because Dad is away. At least the pie will only be divided amongst three of us, unless Mum wants to save a slice for when Dad comes back. I had better top up on school dinner, just in case.

I wonder what vegetables we will be having with it. Carrots I guess –so that we can all see better in the dark.

I like carrots, and peas. But my favourites - Laura says I am weird - are broad beans. We usually have them with ham and parsley sauce. I don't really like the parsley sauce, but the broad beans make up for it. Dad grows them in the garden. He grows a lot of stuff there. Some of it is really nice and some of it's not. Sometimes he lets me help him in the garden. Every year we put up the bamboo canes for the runner beans, and the nets for the strawberries. He doesn't let me help with the glass panes for the marrows because they are dangerous.

Marrows are horrible. I don't know why he grows them, but he does. And when they are ready we have roast marrow on a Sunday. I hate it, but I have to eat it. I am always still at the table long after everyone else has finished, slowly pushing the marrow around my plate with a fork and around my mouth with my tongue. Just thinking about the taste of it makes me shudder. I load the last bit of my toast, get up, and put the plate in the sink.

We bought a dishwasher last year with some money that Grandma left us. Mum was really excited. It is Dad's job to load it but before that everything has to be rinsed and when it is finished everything has to be dried. I am not sure what the dishwasher actually does but Mum had been very keen to get one.

Laura is sometimes allowed to load and empty the dishwasher, but I am restricted to less complicated tasks – I put the rubbish out on Tuesday and clean everyone's shoes on a Sunday night. With my new shoes the cleaning had been much easier last Sunday.

Maybe I should always get new shoes rather than cleaning the old ones? Maybe we should get new plates rather than washing the old ones? That would be cool. But I guess it would cost a lot. But, if we owned a shoe or a plate factory, that would be great. We don't, so I guess we should stick to cleaning and washing.

Who does own the shoe and the plate factories? And do they just replace their shoes and plates rather than washing them? I would, if I owned the factory. That way, as well as saving time spent on the tasks, you could have new shoes or new plates every week. And people would know you were rich.

Everyone at school says that John Andrews's father is rich – he lives in a house that has a swimming pool and his dad drives a Rolls Royce, and they go on holiday to Spain in the summer. Not to the Gower.

But money doesn't make you happy. That's what Mum and Dad say.

John seems happy enough. He is really popular at school. He is the captain of the football team. He isn't actually very good, at least I don't think so, but people always pass the ball to him and he hangs out near the goal where he can score more easily. I am a defender, trying to stop the other team's goal hangers from scoring. In our last match I did really well in the first half but was still substituted at half time and replaced by Stephen Harris. He wasn't very good either and we ended up losing three one.

"Get in the car."

"OK, Mum, just coming now."

I grab my satchel and go outside. The car is on the drive. It isn't a Rolls Royce, but it is quite new. We all went to the garage when Dad bought it. It's called a Beetle. And it's orange!

Laura is already sat in the front. I open the door and get in. Waiting for Mum. She comes out of the front door, locks it and gets in. She starts the car and looks back at me.

"Where's your kitbag? Wait there!" she says and gets back out of the car. A minute later she is back. "Here," she says, handing it to me, "try not to lose any of your kit today."

We set off.

***

Mum drops me off first. Laura goes to a different school. I will get to go there when I am older, Mum says, if I do well in my exams next year, but Laura will be gone to university by then.

I like my school though. I have some good friends there and we get to do some fun things. And today I have football after school. So, it's going to be a good day.

"Hey Joe," someone calls out. I turn round. It's Adrian.

"Hey Ade."

"Have you done your maths homework?' he asks.

"Yes."

"Give it to me so I can copy it."

I get it out of my bag and hand it over.

"You will give it back won't you?" I ask.

"Sure," he says, and laughs as he disappears off to a classroom to copy my answers.

I don't mind Adrian copying my homework. Adrian isn't the only one. But sometimes, unlike the others, he doesn't give it back after he has copied it. He thinks it is funny to keep it. It isn't. Hopefully he will give me my maths back today – I think I have got them all right.

I look around the playground. I have half an hour until school starts. There is a game of football going on by the dining hall but none of my friends are playing. A group of girls are sat on the benches outside the assembly hall, chatting and laughing. They are in my class, but I have never spoken to most of them. There are girls and boys at my school, but we don't mix much, unless you have a sister, then you are allowed to talk to her. But Laura was already at big school when I got here.

27

The other group you aren't supposed to talk to is the teachers. If they come up to talk to you then you don't have any choice but seeking them out to talk to them is not good. I actually quite like most of the teachers

Miss Evans, our class tutor, is my favourite. She has been at the school ever since I started. She teaches English and is often suggesting new books for me to read. I am reading one now, involving Japanese samurai and dragons, it's really good. At the weekend, I spend many hours wielding my katana, defending my family from the dragons. I wonder whether I will ever be brave enough to commit "hara-kiri"?

I wonder how old Miss Evans is? She isn't as old as Mum, but she has been at the school a long time. She's quite young though, I think. But most of the teachers at the school aren't.

They are mainly men and really old. The Headmaster, Dr Crabb (he does sort of walk sideways), looks too old to still be alive, let alone running a school, but he seems to keep going. I have only spoken to Dr Crabb twice. Once when I got a prize for an essay about bees, and the other time when I was caned. It wasn't really fair. It wasn't my fault.

It had not been a good day anyway. It had been raining so we weren't allowed out during breaks. Adrian had kept my homework so that I couldn't hand it in – although I think Mr. Phillips knew that I had done it. During lunch break, after we had our lunch, we had been kept in one of the classrooms because of the rain. Some of the others had started messing around with Nigel and had stolen Nigel's satchel. They were throwing it around while he chased after it. He was upset, crying almost, but no-one tried to help him.

I wasn't going to help but I didn't really want to tease him either. When the satchel came to me, I thought about handing it back to Nigel but instead joined in the game. Just as the satchel arrived with me for the third time, Miss Evans entered the classroom and Nigel burst into tears.

Lots of the boys had been involved but Nigel wasn't going to name them, nor was I –you didn't do that – so my favourite teacher took me to the headmaster's office where I was caned. Dr Crabb explained that it gave him no pleasure to be doing this and that he was surprised to see me there in front of him but that bullying could not be tolerated under any circumstances.

I didn't tell Mum, but I did not know that the school always sent a note to your parents when you were caned. So, I was punished again – this time with a wooden spoon rather than a cane. This didn't seem fair. I didn't get another prize at home for my bee essay, but I did get another caning, why was that?

Mum often says to me "Life is not fair Joseph; you just need to get on with it."

I am never sure whether she means my life is going to be unfair forever or whether everybody's is. At least if it was everybody then that was less unfair?

Miss Evans interrupts my train of thought.

"How are you Joseph? How's the book you are reading?"

"I'm fine Miss, and I really like the book. I have nearly finished it."

"That's good to hear; I know how much you like to read, and it is always a pleasure to see others enjoying literature. How is your sister?"

"She is fine too. She is playing in a music festival next weekend in London."

"Yes, she is very talented at music. You could be too. See you in class in ten minutes?"

"Yes, miss."

Like Laura, I had started playing the piano when I was younger. But I was not as good as her, so I was allowed to stop, once I had passed my Grade One piano exam. Laura had Grade

Eight in Piano and Violin, though, so she was really good. If I could be really good at something I would want it to be reading or sport. If I could, I would make it sport. Reading is not so cool. I had better try hard in football this evening.

Ten minutes to the bell. Where is Adrian with my maths, where are my friends? I will go inside and use the toilet before class begins.

19 September 1972

I had my first cigarette when I was eleven years old. My parents smoked so I was of the view that it was acceptable. My friend Adrian wanted to date a girl – Hayley I think she was called - so I was to look after her friend, Jayne. We met the girls in the park, hung out by the swings, and talked. Before we got there, though, my mate bought ten cigarettes and we arrived at the swings smoking: looking really cool.

My plans to be cool were thwarted in the short term by my early enthusiastic consumption being spotted by a neighbour, who shopped me to my parents. They, despite their own consumption, ruled out smoking until I get old enough to say no to them, and to cigarettes again.

11 December 1973

"Joe, you're late. I gave your round to Charlie; he was here on time."

I knew he would do that, but Mum had insisted I came to the shop even so.

"Yes, sorry Mr. French, is there anything I can do to help?" I ask

"Yes, you can make up these magazines for customers to collect and then bundle up yesterday's unsolds. They're over there."

30

I have done both these jobs before, I have been late before, although not too often. At least he hasn't just sent me home, then I would not have been paid, and that would mean yet another week's delay to the Thin Lizzy album I was saving up for.

That is how I get through my paper round. I work out how many papers I have to deliver to get a track on the album/chapter of the book/copy of the comic I am planning to buy. This morning's work should earn me the rest of The Boys are Back in Town. It would also avoid another run in with the dogs of the local village as I cycled round with their papers. Although there would be no more run ins with Devil Dog (not its real name).

My first encounter with Devil Dog had been in January. The paper round was miserable enough, despite me measuring the rewards I was earning, and in winter it was dark and cold and, sometimes, as that day, icy. I had finished my round and was returning the bag to Mr. French's shop before going home. I parked my bike by the wall and walked towards the shop. There was a large sliver of ice in front of me. I took a footballer swing at it and sent it flying.... into the side of Devil Dog. It yelped, turned to look in my direction and growled. It was on a lead so its owner kept hold of it, otherwise I think I would have been mauled to death.

"Hey!" he shouted (the man not the dog, it was a devil dog but not in a talking in voices way), "why did you do that?" and bent down to comfort the dog.

"Sorry, I didn't see him." (I did not know the gender, but I doubt whether a female dog would be as mean as this one turned out to be for the next ten months). I didn't really like dogs even then but thought I should try and apologise to it. I made my way to them and went to pat him. The dog snarled, baring its teeth.

"You'd better leave it," his owner said. That worked for

me and I was going to turn in to the shop when the dog leapt at me (I think the owner let the lead loosen up but maybe not) and it buried its teeth into my shoulder. Luckily, I was wearing a thick coat for the cold and all he did was tear a hole in the coat. The man pulled him back and I walked (ran) into the shop.

I did not tell my Mum, as it was a new winter coat, and I did not want to get into trouble. With hindsight, maybe if I had told her, she would have sorted it out with the Dog's owner, and it would have been over. As it was, Devil Dog was on my route. I had to deliver to his house. Every day, and I mean every day, when I pushed the morning paper through the letterbox, Devil Dog would throw himself at the front door roaring and growling at me. Although it happened every day, and I tried to anticipate it, he terrified me every time.

Occasionally, particularly as it got lighter in the mornings, Devil Dog would be in the front garden rather than the house. Well, that meant his owners got no paper. I think they worked it out because it did not happen very often. Nor did I ever get a complaint from Mr. French that Number 62's paper had not been delivered, so they probably knew how badly behaved their dog could be. The last time was now about a month ago.

I turned the corner and there he was, in the front garden. I stopped and looked, he glared and growled and then, with little warning, started trying to scrabble over the front wall. He had never done this before, but the wall must be twice his height, so it wasn't going to happen...was it? If I had thought it could, I would have been off, and maybe Devil Dog would still be alive. But I was fascinated by his efforts and when one of them came off, it was too late to be out of harm's way. I jumped on my bike and set off, Devil Dog in pursuit barking and growling. We rounded the corner and I narrowly missed Doctor Jones' car, travelling a bit too fast. The dog was not so lucky, although in my mind not the greatest sadness, and it was hit hard and with a crunch.

Doctor Jones stopped, got out, asked if I was OK, and tried to tend to Devil Dog. I, in no mood to hang around, sped off. Devil Dog was not on my round again (except in the occasional paper round nightmare) so I assume he was put down.

Although I can't remember, we entered the EU, the Americans lost the Vietnam War, Laura left home, and Elvis Presley died.

6 April 1978

"Right, guys, we need this one."

We are in the changing room at Bridgend School. It's the third round of the Schools Cup. We got to the semi-finals last year. No thanks to me though. This is my first time in the team. Alun Jones is injured so I am coming in as number eight. This is my chance for glory on the rugby pitch!

"Get out there and start quickly. Last time we played them they had two tries before you lot started playing!"

"Yes sir!" we shout.

We all want to do well for 'Sir'. He has a Welsh cap. It doesn't get much more impressive than that (well, more than one cap would be I guess, but one is more than most of us will ever get). The school closed for the day to celebrate when he got it.

"Sandpiper."

"Yes, sir."

"Just get the first few tackles in, and don't let them push our scrum backwards."

I nod at him. I am not sure I can speak, even if he expects me to. I have been thinking about this game all week and now it's here, I want to be strong and confident. I am,

33

though, feeling a little weak, and nervous. I have already been to the loo twice since we got here.

The second time, I bump into one of their players on the way out. He is huge, twice my size. I am tall but slender (skinny is how people describe me). This guy is my height but everything else is just a multiple, his arms, chest, his legs are the same size as my waist. Let's hope he can't run fast.

He can.

We're only fifteen minutes into the match and, again, they are up two tries to nil. It's not just him. Their scrum is bigger than ours and we are being pushed back every time. We are their equals at the line out. Partly, I like to think, through my contribution, but we are going to struggle to get into their half. At least there, Stephen can try and kick a penalty or a drop goal. Their try line looks a long way away.

So, Stephen kicks off again. High and wide, my side of the pitch. I am going to run with enthusiasm and try and catch the ball or, at least, tackle their guy when he does. I manage the latter, and to bundle him into touch with the ball. Our line out. Our captain, Jon, slaps me on the back.

"Good one Joe, now win us the ball."

We line up, not really straight, but nor are they and, at this level, referees are realistic about how straight the throw in at the line out, or put in at the scrum, is expected to be.

The ball comes in, I leap, with assistance, and grab the ball, turning to face my teammates as I land, and we start to push. This is the nearest we have been to their try line with the ball all match. We need to make it count. I think we all know that, as we are pushing them backwards for the first time. The inevitable rolling maul collapse happens (we would do the same, and have already).

Rugby has some great terminology – a rolling maul, like some sort of mobile scrap, tries, rucks, hookers, props, spear tackles (not a good thing to do), the much-used phrase

34

'hospital pass' (the pass which ends with you catching the ball then an ambulance to the hospital). All great poetry which, mixed with our songs, is one of the things that being Welsh is all about. Although, to be fair the rugby words are all English! Not though, our songs. Not us for us 'The flower of Scotland', in English! No, we sing 'Hen Wlad Fy Nhadau', 'Calon Lan', 'Ar Hyd y Nos' (OK, enough Welsh now), 'Cwm Rhondda', most people know that as 'Bread of Heaven', that's one that has ended up in English.

No time for songs now, it's a penalty to us. We should really kick it and get some points on the board. But our tails are up, and Stephen takes a quick one. They aren't expecting that, and he makes some good yards before he is brought down. Tom picks up the ball and passes to his left, to me.

My moment! Do I go for the line or pass it further left? The line it is, or should be, but not in this case. 'Man Mountain' from the toilets looms large in front of me.

Time stops as he flattens me. People said afterwards that he didn't actually tackle me, I just ran into him and bounced off and on to the ground. I still have enough sense to roll back and place the ball our side when he lands his full weight, through his right leg, onto my left hand. I still think I can see the marks nowadays, just below my knuckles. I can certainly still remember the pain. I don't think I passed out, but it would have been a smart move.

The referee blows for my injury.

I am trying not to scream, or cry but it fucking hurts! Ow! Ow!

Sir's assistant comes onto the pitch.

"That doesn't look good," he says, looking at my hand. I don't want to look, just in case, although I am not sure I can actually see at the moment.

"He'd better come off ref, it looks like something's broken."

35

Something was. Or, in fact several things. Who knew I had 27 bones in my hand? And ten of them are in trouble. My middle finger is still crooked even now.

While I went off to A&E, we scored from the resultant penalty but lost 19 - 11 in the end. Although the school didn't close for a day to remember my near triumph and personal sacrifice, I did get to carry my wounded hand as a badge of honour for a few weeks.

By the time my hand had healed, so had Alun Jones, and I returned to the occasional B team appearance.

22 May 1978

"This one's called "Balls to the Neighbours", says Robin, and I start ('lay down' technically, but this was punk, so no one did any technical stuff) the drum rhythm. Robin starts shouting into the microphone, Dave thrashes his guitar and the crowd watch. Is twenty people a crowd, and are you part of the crowd if you are sat having a drink in the pub we're playing?

We are Cosmopolitan, a three piece, post punk, boy band. Think 'The Piranhas', but without much talent, a decent following or a recording contract. We did a cover of their Virginity, a cool version of Wuthering Heights, and our own stuff like 'Balls'. We also did some very bad (but should it be good?) crowd pleasing Sex Pistols, even though we claimed to be "post punk".

I bought a rudimentary second-hand drum kit for £50 (a lot of papers delivered), never learnt to play it but the qualification for being in a band was seldom any higher than owning the relevant equipment. With my drums, I was soon in demand from several competing drummerless bands. My chosen band mates, Robin on vocals, and our guitarist, Dave, are, like me, some of the least cosmopolitan people you will ever meet but we like the name and Robin's mum reads the magazine.

Robin is from Luton originally, like me. Dave is actually properly Welsh, from Neath. They are both clever, but lazy, pupils, affording them endless time to sleep, drink and rehearse. The studious half of my personality makes a few more demands on my time. So, I sleep less to keep up with their drinking and Cosmopolitan rehearsal time. It seems to work.

We all have similar musical tastes, which helps, although Dave is the longest standing music fan and most knowledgeable by far. He occasionally forces us to listen to his King Crimson, Henry Cow and Frank Zappa and while are very rude about this retro self-indulgent stuff, there is something to it, particularly after a few pints.

As a deservedly unproud owner of the Commodores Three Times a Lady as my first ever purchased single – don't ask, someone I like liked it, but they didn't like me – I mostly leave the song writing to Dave and Robin.

I did, whoever, provide some memorable lyrics to our (every respectable band had one) anti-war song.

In the Army

Join the professionals
Blown up in Belfast
You died for some bastard
And his political ideals

Territorial Army
Hitler Youth
Or old men
With a desire
To die for something
We fought two wars this century

37

Said we'd never fight again
But the memories fade now
And we glorify our dead men

Remembrance Sunday
What a load of shit
Two minutes silence
Wearing poppies

Pretty flowers
For pretty pictures
Of men dying for their country

Guts spilling out over Passchendaele
Severed limbs
Symbols of war
Glory to this country
And it's fucked up mentality

We played a handful of gigs, to a (largish) handful of people, were usually paid in drink and I lost my drum kit when a rival band trashed it during the Christmas holidays. So, we never got far, or a recording contract, but I still have the posters from our gigs, a pair of my drumsticks and, in the midst of what turned out to be our farewell performance, I felt like a rock star.

11 September 1979

"So, you want us to stay away for the whole night?" asks Mum.

"Yes, you did when Laura had her eighteenth!"

"Yes, but she had three girlfriends round for dinner, you are talking about having a full-blown party. What do you think, Owen?"

"You do understand that the house and whole thing will be your responsibility?" says Dad, unusually sternly.

"Yes."

"Well then I would let him, we can go and stay somewhere nice for the night, we don't get away much on our own."

"What about Laura?"

"I am sure she won't actually want to come to a kids' party. She'll come down from London for your actual birthday though I hope."

Kids? I am about to be 18, and a bona fide adult, although probably not yet as fully formed as Laura had been at my age.

Anyway, the party is on!

I call Jane that night to let her know. She put me up to it. We are 'sort of dating' although I think I am probably dating more than she is. I do really like her. I wrote a poem about how cool she is. She is cool and, so, by association, am I. Plus if Jane invites her friends then the party will be really popular. Jane had been dating my bandmate Robin before me, so she had come to some of the Cosmopolitan band rehearsals. She told me that Robin and she had had a huge row and he had dumped her. To be fair, Robin didn't seem to mind me hanging out with her.

Mum and Dad leave on the Saturday afternoon and Jane comes round to help set things up. She looks amazing and I spend the afternoon following her round, taking instructions. Much of my music – Bowie, T Rex, and Thin Lizzy - is discarded in favour of her more poppy stuff – and every Roxy Music album ever made. She has a thing for Bryan Ferry, and lot of others too, actually. She puts Virginia Plain on the tape player while we (I) carry in the beer (purchased by Dad) from the garage.

Jane goes home to change. I have a bath and put on my coolest clothes – the flares, the velvet jacket and the wide collar shirt. I find a pack of condoms in my jacket pocket. I haven't bought them! Maybe Jane had snuck them in there while I wasn't looking?

Word has got around town that there is a parent free house party taking place and by nine my ten friends and at least one hundred people I know only vaguely (although Jane seems to know them all), have descended. The attendees even include half a visiting Canadian rugby team which gives rise to an impromptu game of sevens in the back garden. The game is eventually suspended when, after the second of my two rugby balls has sailed over the fence at the back, the replacement full lager can cuts one of the Canadians above his eye.

When we get back inside, I try to find Jane. I ask a couple of her friends who say they do not know. I find Robin, has he seen her. He thinks she has gone off somewhere with John Andrews.

Jane has gone off with John Andrews, although she has not gone far. They have had sex in my parents' bed. John left quickly afterwards, embarrassed presumably (hopefully, the least he can do), but Jane hung around. While I consoled myself by drinking even more and dancing wildly to Thin Lizzy.

After everyone else has gone, Jane came and sat on my lap.

"What do you want?" I ask.

"You," she says.

"No, you don't."

"John was nothing. It's you I want."

"No, you don't."

"Do you love me"?

"Sadly yes."

"Read me that poem you wrote about me. Let's go and read it in bed."

We move to the scene of her crime and I read "She" out loud:

40

She
Partial happiness
Heroes
Aspire

Deeper than before
Do not understand
Then the sympathy
Understanding fails

She
Subtlety
Or distance
Charm
Poser is this time
Strange
Weird Normality

Irreverent
Life is fun
Or what?

Jane asks me what it means.

"It means I love you, but I am scared you don't love me."

She climbs on top of me, but I, gently, move her off.

"Let's just go to sleep," I say.

She is gone in the morning when I wake.

I make an effort to tidy up the worst of the mess but am still in the midst of it when my parents arrive home. They don't seem to mind and muck in, even Mum.

Later that day Dad comes up to me.

"Mum found this in our bed," he says, holding up a dangly earring. "Do you know anything about it?"

I smile sheepishly. And Dad smiles back.

"Perhaps you want to return it to its owner?"

I never do. I keep it for a few months and then throw it in the sea.

A few years later, Dad tells me that it had been him who put the condoms in my jacket pocket.

5 December 1979

We are at a Damned gig in Cardiff.

It is a great gig, although the support act, Victim, make me realise that punk sometimes takes the no need to know how to play your instruments or even make a recognisable noise to inaccessible levels. No matter, The Damned are amazing. And we are buzzing as we make our way back to the train station, even though it is bitterly cold.

There is no school tomorrow, which is fortunate, given the amount we have drunk and the fact that we missed the last train. We now have to wait until the 5 am train, along with several hundred others. As the drink wears off and the time wears on, it gets really cold. We are not really dressed for the outdoors, more for punk style. At some point, maybe one or two in the morning, lots of newspapers, piles of them, are dropped off in the station. I guess they were for the shops there, or for the first trains out?

Temptation gets the better of me, and a few others, and we cut open several bundles to wrap ourselves in.

It must be then that the frustrated arsonist memory kicked in. I pile a few of the papers up and light them. Fellow travellers join me around the fire. Of course, it gets out of hand, as more papers are brought and more…

I think a fire alarm went off first but maybe not. Anyway, within minutes the fire brigade arrived. It was easy to extinguish but what I hadn't reckoned on (reckoned, there was

42

no reckoning involved) was the arrival of dozens of riot police with, wait for it, dogs. Big, straining at the leash, bite your arm dogs. I guess with hindsight, a couple of hundred punks setting fire to a railway station merits a decent response but it took us all a bit by surprise.

Any residual sobering up is done quickly. I have just applied to university. Being done for arson is going to presumably be in their list of things to take into account in considering my application.

The police have us line up along a platform edge. What are they going to do, push us onto the tracks, or under a train?

"Did you see who started it?"

"Where do you live?"

"Show me some ID."

"Wipe that smile off your face."

No smiling on mine. Several of the crowd have seen me start things off. Do I think I would have told on me if I was them? Probably, this is scary. This isn't your mum asking who stole the last biscuit from the tin. This is serious stuff. I like to think that the 'us and them' culture of the punk movement prevailed. The police go down the whole line, asking after the culprit, who started it? No-one blabs. It is like the Spartacus movie. Except that in this case "I'm not Spartacus" was the constant refrain, all the way down the line, with the occasional glance at Kirk (me). Clearly there was only one option, they would have to arrest us all. That would have been a disaster for me personally, but I think they worked out that two hundred punks in front of magistrates on a Monday morning was not going to help the city's image.

We were taken back to Bridgend on a specially scheduled train, accompanied by Wales' finest and greeted by some more when we arrived, but it could have been a lot worse.

18 June 1980

It is Jonathan Forsyth's 18th birthday, and he has booked the Paradise club on the seafront for his party. I have been there before but not for an 18th. Jonathan is one of the youngest in our year so his is one of the last 18th parties I am going to. I wonder whether my parents would have preferred me to have it here, but I bet it costs a lot.

Despite my punk credentials, I am going wearing my finest Thin Lizzy get up. Not quite capable of the Phil Lynott hairdo, I still go for the rest of the look in a big way, including the ubiquitous clip-on earring. It is the only stylish set of clothes I have, bought with Mum (after a long debate) in Cardiff a few months earlier. This is their second outing, the first was drumming at Cosmopolitan's gig at the school festival.

Dad drops me off, tells me not to drink too much and gives me a tenner.

"Let me know if you need picking up. And if you are going to come in drunk, just go straight to bed."

"Will do, Dad."

Although he drops me off at the club, no one is going to be there yet; we are all meeting in the Red Crown first. The beer is cheaper, and you can go in and out, whereas when we are in the club, we can't leave and return.

The Red Crown is packed, and it takes ages to be served. I am buying a round for Robin and Dave, my fellow band members, and one for Jonathan, as it is his birthday. Although, if he drinks all the pints he has been bought he will probably end up in A&E having his stomach pumped. That happened to John Andrews at one of his parties. I wasn't at the party, but someone told me.

Eventually I get served but we decide that we will trade the cheaper beer for the less crowded, or maybe better staffed, bar at the club for our next round. Our band had offered to play at Jonathan's party. We offered to do it for free, for the publicity, but apparently the club would have charged a lot for set up and sound checks and stuff, so he just had a DJ. We had written a song about it, inevitably entitled "Banned from Paradise".

The bar is, as we had hoped, much quieter when we get into the club and I get another round of drinks. I had made the mistake of telling Robin and Dave that my dad had given me a tenner and they had decided it was for the three of us.

We grab a table away from the dance floor. It's not our thing. We think we are too cool to dance to another band's music, although we love many of the songs the DJ plays that night.

Robin does eventually get a round in and his older brother, Eric, comes to sit with us. He has his girlfriend Lesley with him. I have met them before, but tonight I decide that Lesley is one of the most attractive women I have ever met, or so my three pints of beer tell me. Attached to Robin's elder brother and out of my league but just being around her makes me feel good.

Eric gives me some money for the next round – he works and has his own money. I go to the bar, which, by now, is busier, as the remainder of the Red Crown crowd have arrived.

"Do you want to buy me a drink," one of the new arrivals asks.

"Sure, what would you like?" I say, without looking at her.

"A snowball," she says, and I turn to look at her.

She is pretty.

"What's a snowball?" I ask

She smiles. "The barman will know," she says and lights a cigarette.

"Do you want one?"

45

"Sure."

She hands me her lit one and lights up another.

"Thanks"

"My name's Joanne," she says, "people call me Jo. I saw you drumming at the school concert, you were pretty good."

"Thanks!" I try to sound casual, but I know the look on my face is probably giving away my feelings. "I haven't seen you before, are you in my year?"

"No, I joined this year, in lower sixth, I was at Cowbridge Girls before that."

"Who's next?" asks the barmaid.

"I am," I say, "can I have three pints of bitter, a coke, a glass of white wine and a snowball."

I leave my beer with her snowball on the bar and take the other drinks back to the table. I was going to go back to the bar but before I can Jo brings the drinks over to the table and sits down.

"Hi everyone, I'm Jo," she says and clinks glasses with them all. I am in love.

I meet Jonathan in the toilet a bit later. He has clearly had a few of the drinks that everyone bought him and manages to keep going at the urinal for the time it takes me to unzip, urinate, zip, wash and dry my hands, even though he had already been in full flow when I arrived. He eventually finishes and, wiping his hands on his jeans, beckons to me.

"That girl you are with, do you know who she is?"

"Jo."

"Yes, but do you know who she is, whose girlfriend she is?"

"She's got a boyfriend?"

"Well, I think they finished but very recently. But she was dating Max."

"Max?"

46

'You know, the captain of the rugby team."

So, it appears that I am entering into a prom cliché!

"Well, if they've broken up."

"Sure, but apparently she finished it and now he's out to get anyone he sees her with."

"Is he here?"

"He just arrived."

What am I going to do now? I can leave, or I can leave Jo alone, or I can get my head kicked in by Max, or Jonathan could be exaggerating.

It appears he isn't. Max comes over to our table, "What are you doing with this load of losers" he asks, careful not to include Robin's brother and Lesley in his gaze.

"What's it got to do with you?" asks Jo.

"Yeah, what's it got to with you?" I repeat, in my head, but not out loud.

"Because you were my girlfriend and who you go with reflects badly on me," he says

"Really, don't talk rubbish," Jo replies.

"Find another new boyfriend," he says and walks off.

"Don't worry," she says to me, "you're not my new boyfriend anyway."

She gets up and follows him.

Jonathan comes over, "See," he says, "told you. But don't worry, if he wants a fight there'll be a few of us happy to join in on your side. Although he's got a few mates too."

"Beer?" asks Robin.

"Probably not," I say. I have sobered up pretty quickly.

The evening turns into West Side Story as my Jets and Max's Sharks prowl the club recruiting members, and the girls take themselves off to chat about the idiots that boys can be.

I had a couple of fights when I was much younger, both broken up by teachers before a victor could be declared, and I had been to a few gigs where the dancing turned into fighting, but this was new territory for me. And not one I was necessarily going to fare well in.

I am back in the toilet again.

Paul Davis is in there.

He is well known for fighting (a lot), and usually winning.

"I hear you and Max are going to get it on."

"Give me your earring and I'll fight on your side."

"OK," I say, and unclip and hand it over.

"Let me know when it's on," he snarls and leaves.

So, when is it on? Eric comes into the toilet.

"Look," he says, "this is crazy, someone is going to get hurt. Me and Lesley are going to get you out of here. I am going to get my car, be outside in five minutes."

I go back to the table, finish my beer, have a quick look around for Max and then leave the club. A car pulls up and I get in. Jo is already in the back seat.

We speed off, with Eric and Lesley in the front and me and Jo in the back. Eric drives us down to the beach by the caravan park and goes for a walk with Lesley.

And I lose my virginity, clumsily, quickly, riskily – condom free. I can still conjure up the memory of me and Jo and the sea and sand in the moonlight. It is a useful image for my many lonely nights since.

Apparently, the Jets and the Sharks did get it on, and no-one, not even Max, or somewhat disappointingly, Robin or Dave, noticed that I wasn't there. I was not going to correct the impression created. Nor was Jo. We did not get together again after that night.

18 July 1980

I was left to catch the last one while the rest of them wandered off for breakfast. I am the new boy and anyway only

48

there as a summer job so fair enough. Forcing it into the pen isn't going to be an easy task on my own though. I have enough bruises from earlier in the week to testify to that.

I light up a cigarette and wait. You never know, it might run in there of its own accord. Although it is unlikely, I think they can sense what is happening in the shed and so always flee to the other side of the field. I will try again in a minute.

This is the toughest summer job I have ever had. It is partly self-inflicted. Most of my friends either live off their parents' money –not available; or have internships –not applied for; – or just signed on and didn't bother trying to find work– not achieved. I had gone to the Job Centre to sign on and make myself available for work.

"Do you have a means of transport?" asks the woman at the Centre.

"I have a bike."

She laughs. "We do have something in Bridgend."

"Great," I say.

"Have you worked in an abattoir before?"

"No," I say, taken aback by the idea.

"Let me phone and see if they want experience," she says and steps away from the counter.

How is this going to work out? Is it proper manual labour? Presumably, unless they want me to do the paperwork. While I have never been a great campaigner for animal rights, this is a factory where animals are killed. But only middle-class liberal thinking would reject participation in the death of food yet be comfortable with the eating of it. Surely the politically correct thing will be to experience the creation of the food: it will give me a much more credible point of view.

I am early on in my political development and this has a certain logic. Did Morrissey work in an abattoir before he wrote Meat is Murder? No, he didn't, although to be fair presumably he was a vegetarian.

So, I find myself up against a terrified year-old sheep – lamb really. I find it easier to think of it as a sheep, even if the outcome will actually be called lamb on the shrink-wrapped supermarket trays. I am not actually doing the killing. My job is to help scramble the sheep into the pen at the back of the shed. The regulars will hoist them up and the next time I see them they are recognisably what we can all see hanging in a traditional butchers' shop, a halved headless skinned, innardless side of lamb.

My other job is to pressure hose the carcasses to clean them and then to roll them through on the hook system to the freezer area out the back. There are two other guys on the hoses –Dai and Euan, they are full time and have both been working here for six months now. In that time, they have become immune to the stench of the place, to the freshest breakfasts I have ever had (as the offal was fried seconds after it became offal) and to the fact that the place didn't actually stun the sheep, they just had their throats cut and bled out as they went along the conveyor.

I had not become immune and was not there long enough to discover if I ever would have. My lack of immunity meant that I went down with some sort of sheep disease – foot and mouth? – which had the GP also recommending I be quarantined. The GP did, though, sign me off medically, allowing me not to return but still get my money. I did not eat lamb for several years after that without the smell taking me back to the abattoir.

I vowed to try and study energetically at university so that I could work less hard in the future.

50

PART TWO - WORK AND WOMEN

1981 to 2000

I did work (and play) hard at university and got a first-class law degree. While I was there, we won the Falklands War, John Lennon and Ronald Reagan were shot and the SDP was founded.

After university, I got my first (and, as it turned out, only) proper job. In London.

24 June 1986

It is morning again, twenty-four hours since the last, a fact verified noisily by the alarm at the side of my bed. As the alarm crescendos to enough decibels, I open my eyes.

I cannot see the sun. That does not worry me, as I know it is there, behind the clouds. All the same, it would be nice to see it, just to reassure me. I have woken in one of those moods – brought on by a weird and sad dream – where I need lots of reassurance and seeing the sun would help. Things are not going well at the moment. I feel as if can't remember when they last have; perhaps never. Although I know that isn't true. I try to think of the last time I hadn't felt like this, but it eludes me. I can remember lots of times when, like now, things felt like they were going badly, but the good times –none come to mind. It strikes me that this is naturally so, that one only notices the bad times. This seems to fit my impression of others, that no one is really ever happy, just miserable or, maybe, neither miserable nor happy. The discovery of this universal law cheers me slightly – it means that no one else is happy either, even if most of them aren't as miserable as me.

Self-indulgent and negative thinking over, I raise my

head from the pillow and prop myself up on one elbow. From this position, I can reach the packet of cigarettes that lie on a small table on the far side of my bed. Removing one with my teeth, I replace the packet, and exchange it for a book of matches. Once I have lit the cigarette, I remove it from my lips and sink back to the horizontal.

For a long time now, this has been my first ritual of the day, the pre-reveille cigarette. Despite my constant indulgence, however, it does not put me at peace with the world, nor does it set me up for the day, it just gives me a headache. I often wonder why I do not give them up, but I have never seriously attempted to do so. So far, I've managed to avoid serious illness, but of course I am still too young to believe that such a fate would ever await me. I know, if I admit it to myself, that I would save money if I stopped smoking, and this is something much more real to me, but the financial saving is not immediate enough, unlike deciding not to buy a new car or not to go on an expensive foreign holiday, decisions I have made many times.

While I am musing over the habit, I smoke my cigarette, pulling hard on its end and blowing the smoke upwards. If the sun was out, the smoke would be visible, a pale, thin cloud hanging from the ceiling. Instead, I can see the ceiling itself, with its polystyrene tiles and garish light shade. Now and then, one of the tiles will gently float down and wait for me to glue it back into place. Perhaps it is the smoke; maybe the heat melts the glue. At the moment, though, all the tiles are in place, so I shift my gaze to the rest of the room.

Draped over a chair at the end of my bed is my jacket, the rest of my clothes discarded in a pile by its side. The furniture in the room is, I suppose, typical of any accommodation rented for £200 a month. A solid wooden wardrobe stands in one corner, a large table in the other. Below the table are two boxes of books and magazines. I read a lot. I think. Perhaps too much. Or maybe it is just that I read the wrong things. Either way, I do not read for pleasure. On the far side of the bed is the small table on which lie my cigarettes and matches, along with my alarm clock and ashtray. Beyond this is a small dressing table, topped by a large mirror, which, from the angle at which I am lying, contains an image of the wardrobe opposite.

Glancing back at the clock, I lean over and stub out the remains of my cigarette in the cluttered ashtray. I hardly ever empty the ashtrays; I just leave them until they are piled so high that they are impossible to use without creating a small fire. Then they receive the full treatment – they are emptied, washed thoroughly, dried and returned to post, ready for the ashes of the next week or so. This one, however, will last a couple more days at least.

The glance at the clock tells me it is time to get up and, having finished my cigarette, I now have no excuse. I never like getting up. It's not the actual physical effort, nor the fact that it means I can't sleep any more. Rather, it's the significance as the start of the day. In my present mood I am not looking forward to next fifteen hours or so. Having set my feet on the floor, though, I can't turn back and, rising on them, I wrap myself in a towel and set off for the bathroom.

On the way I stop to turn on the radio in the kitchen. The bathroom sits at the opposite end of a short passage from my bedroom, with the kitchen inhabiting the space in between. These three rooms, converted from the first floor of what could not have been a particularly spacious residence overall – "modest" or "compact" would have been the agent's description – represent my entire living space. The sizes of the bathroom and kitchen are probably best described as of minimum utility. I can't swing a cat in either, but I can probably manage a flannel in the bathroom and a small saucepan in the kitchen. The bedroom is bigger but as, if I am neither cooking nor washing, it is "home", I do not consider it to be overly large. I have thought about moving many times but have never managed to find anywhere better at an affordable rent. So, I have stayed here and paid my rent regularly, ever since I came down to London, three years ago.

Reaching the end of the passage, I push open the bathroom door. It only opens halfway before colliding with the basin behind. When I first moved in, this had been really irritating and I have tried various solutions. A doorstop only narrows the entrance further, while anything attached to the basin soon falls off. I thought about cutting a basin sized hole in the door but wasn't sure my landlord would approve, and it did not take me long to conclude that it was less trouble to enter the bathroom sideways. I do that today and, once inside, fill the basin with water – cold, of course – I do not consider it prudent economics to use 30 minutes electricity for a warm wash. Nor am I into this new thing of having a shower every day. There is a shower in the bathroom, or, at least, a shower attachment over the bath, but our parents brought us up to have a bath every Sunday and that's good enough for me. I wash quickly, dousing my face, finally waking up properly. Despite the cold water, I manage to shave, empty the basin and dry myself and slide back out of the bathroom.

Returning to the bedroom, I begin to get dressed, managing to find the last of my clean and ironed shirts at the back of the wardrobe. Like the ashtrays, I leave the washing of clothes as long as possible; it is not a task I love. Every two weeks or so I will take a trip to the launderette, fifteen minutes' walk away. For a small extra charge, I could leave my clothes for a service wash, but I never do so – I have few enough clothes as it is, without somebody losing half of them for me. The launderette is one of my least favourite places. There is never anywhere to sit. The ratio of chairs to machines and, therefore, customers is never more than one to five and, no matter what the time of day, it is always full. Nor is there anything to do. No one ever speaks, they are always deep in their own concentration – willing the time to pass more quickly or someone's jeans to dry this time. Despite the nearness of my flat, I never go back there while my clothes wash. Again, I fear someone will steal them, or at least unload them onto the floor – everyone in the launderette seems so hostile.

Despite all this, I will have to go there at the weekend and, I make a mental note – even going so far as putting yesterday's clothes in the laundry bag in readiness. I finish dressing. Picking up my jacket from the back of the chair, I brush it down quickly and, collecting my cigarettes and matches, leave the room.

Moments later – it is not a long walk – I arrive in the kitchen and turn the radio down a bit. I love music. Almost all music; but not quite all. The station is playing one of those awful tunes sung by a sickeningly good-looking group who seem to be cheerful all the time. Probably because they are in a band. I have always wanted to be in band – was for a couple of years – but then had to go to university so I could "get a proper job" – I was the drummer. Not a very good one. I never had a lesson. I took the "punk" spirit of not being able to play your instrument to heart, even though, as I discovered later, many of the punks had been to art school or the Royal College of Music. But even my band's stuff is much better than this rubbish on the radio. I turn it down even further.

Now that the music is slightly less annoying, I deposit my jacket and cigarettes on the kitchen table, light a cigarette, place it in another crowded ashtray and pick up the kettle. The kettle is already full, so I light the stove. In the time it will take the kettle to boil, I hope to find a clean mug and spoon, and coffee, milk and sugar – breakfast. I open the fridge and, as expected, there is no milk, the sole occupant being some hardening cheddar. Black coffee then, and a trip to the supermarket tomorrow.

So, tomorrow isn't going to be a great day, laundry and shopping! At least people aren't as hostile in the supermarket, and you don't need a chair. I always go to the same supermarket; they know me there. Things seem OK price wise and they have the basic stuff a young person needs. Another supermarket has opened recently nearer to the flat. I went there once but it is one of those modern "good for you" shops, full of health foods and stuff without preservatives, with a shelf life that means most of the food I buy goes off in the bag on the way home. Not for me.

The kettle starts to whistle before I have assembled the breakfast things but I am soon seated at the table alternating between sips of sugared black coffee and puffs of my cigarette. Health foods indeed.

Stubbing out my cigarette, putting the empty coffee cup in the sink, I pick up my jacket. I check that my keys are in my pocket, and the stove turned off, and leave the room. Seconds later, I am back. I put my cigarettes and matches in my jacket pocket and set off again. This time I will make it to the street below…

***

It is raining. Not a lot, but enough to guarantee that I will be wet by the time I get to the tube station. I don't own an umbrella; I never have done. Everyone else in the street seems to though. It is as much as I can do to avoid being impaled on one of them, as people rush past, heads clad in black roofs, blind to fellow pavement occupiers. Getting wet but not impaled, I arrive at Mornington Crescent station. Someone once told me excitedly that I live near the end of a Radio Four quiz game, they called the "eponymous Mornington Crescent". What does "eponymous" mean? It's one of those words people use at work, like "ubiquitous", where I don't know what it means but I have to pretend and try and join in. I think I have ended up at a firm where everyone else went to Eton or somewhere like that. So, they all know what the Wall Game, the subjunctive and Henley are about. I should have stayed in Wales and worked for the council like my Dad.

Unless I am running late, I usually stop outside the station for a cigarette, but the rain puts a stop to that today. Even though you can smoke on the tube I prefer not to. Sometimes I even travel in the no smoking carriages, although, if I have run out of cigarettes the night before, the smoking carriages are great for your first one of the day. So many people are smoking you can just stand there and breathe it in.

I stop at Sam's to buy the Guardian. 'Morning' is exchanged. And a paper; for 50 pence. No cigarettes needed today.

The paper is full of England's exploits at the World Cup in Mexico. They struggled out of their group but were then robbed by the hand of Maradona, and are on their way home. At least they got there. Wales didn't; it's not even worth asking. The problem with being Welsh, when it comes to football, is that they never get to any of the international tournaments. They went to the World Cup in Sweden before I was born and that has been that. Rugby is the proper Welsh sport of course, but when you live and work in London most normal people want to talk about football. Only posh people talk about rugby and 'Twickers'.

In football, in those conversations, I support Luton Town, because, and this is embarrassing, I was born there. Luton is not particularly embarrassing itself, just a Welshman being born somewhere in England. People argue that I am, therefore, English. I explain that, just as being born on a boat does not make you a fisherman, so being born in England does not force that nationality on me. Even though they are both from Wales, Mum and Dad were working in Luton when they met and married and had me. We soon moved back to Wales and to a proper rugby nation but when I had to choose a football team, I wanted to pick one in the first division. There were no Welsh teams that high up the league at the time and so I went with Luton. I don't go and watch them, but I can talk about what's happening to them from a study of the football pages of the Guardian.

I used to play football at school. You also "had to" play rugby. I would have loved to have been good at it – I did once get to play number eight for the school's first team, and someone trod on my hand – but I wasn't very good at all. Everyone assumes that, because I grew up in Wales, I must have played lots of rugby. They are a bit disappointed if I tell them the truth, so sometimes I don't.

That's never a smart move. It might work in the short term with people you meet once but it can get complicated with people you know well. Exaggerating your rugby career is one thing but some of the more serious stuff, you need to be careful about what stories you have told and remember who you have told them to.

My sex life, such as it is, is a bit of minefield for that. In my head and when talking to friends, I have had several sexual relationships. In practice I had sex once in a caravan park six years ago. The longer this abstinence goes on, the more tempted I am to go back to the caravan park to try and find her.

I have made my way to the platform. "Mind the gap" interrupts me, the tube arrives, and we squeeze on. I recognise some of the passengers as regulars, others look new. They all look damp, like me. When I first came to London and discovered the Tube, I thought it was amazing. I don't have a car or, in fact, a driving licence, so how else would I get around?

The Tube map itself is amazing, like a circuit diagram from my physics classes at school. Here I am travelling from the Mornington Crescent anode to Chancery Lane, down the black wire and then along the red one. Along with my fellow electrons. Do electrons travel from anodes to cathodes? Or the other way round? And if they can only travel in the one direction, how do they get home? Maybe they change into protons at home time?

It is time to change lines, or wires. I don't need to look at the signs. Once you have travelled on the Tube for a while, you know that most of the signs are misleading or just plain wrong. They are just trying to control the traffic. So, when it says, 'No connection to the Central Line this way', it means that way is the shortest route to the other line but that's not the way they want you to go. I furtively peel off from the crowd, not wanting too many others to know my secret, although several regulars follow me.

The tunnel is plastered with movie and theatre show posters. I have already seen Top Gun, along with everyone else. Mona Lisa looks like it could be quite good as does Aliens, although it does not open for a few weeks.

Everyone at work is going on about Les Miserables, a musical about the French Revolution. Mum says she wants to see it next time she and Dad are down in London, but I have no idea how to get tickets. I like music but not musicals. I like movies but not the theatre. In the theatre you can tell that it's just actors in front of scenery. Not in a movie though. Although I guess they are actors, movies feel like real life to me.

Someone bumps into me. A 'Sorry' mumbled over the shoulder that is already disappearing into the carriage. Why can't people wait for everyone to get out first? That won't make room for everyone, but it'll make room for some of us, I think, as I make my own insistent yet – I hope – gentle, progress into the train.

I'm not looking forward to getting to work. Today is feedback day, where I get the results of my appraisal, and they

59

tell me if I've got a bonus and a pay rise. I got both last year but even so, I can't help but feel that it would be much better if they didn't do it this way. What will I do when they decide not to reward me with either? How will I get a new job, or stay there when everyone knows I am no good?

I will get a rise and a bonus today though, because, actually, I am quite good at my job. On the other hand, there are quite a few people in my office who aren't, and yet they get the same financial reward, so the process obviously doesn't work properly. Another reason to scrap it. I'd be happy to do that. I don't need much money. I only have to pay my rent, food, travel and have a few nights out. I get paid more than enough to do that. So, if they stop paying more, I'd be OK. And then I'd stop worrying about whether people who don't deserve it get paid more than me.

That hasn't happened so far. I joined with ten other people. Two have left, and half of the rest of us, including me, are graded highest. One of the others in that group – Elizabeth – is really good. Stuart thinks he is. The other two just spend most of their time messing around but our manager likes them.

I like Elizabeth, and she knows I do, but I have now waited nearly three years for a sign that she likes me or that I should ask her out. We had a drunken snog at a gig last year and she laughs at my jokes. She lives with her parents, near Richmond Park, won a scholarship to a private school, and went to a proper university. All a bit out of my league, but she's really nice.

Anyway, she is on holiday this week. That's relaxed, missing feedback day. She must be confident about the outcome. I wonder where she has gone on holiday and who she's gone with. I once saw her in a nightclub with our managing director, but he's not on holiday this week. He's waiting for me to get in so he can provide feedback.

The same guy who had barged past me on the way into

the carriage pushes past on his way out at Holborn. "Sorry," I say, again. I could get out at Holborn too. It is pretty much equidistant from work, but it is raining so spending more time out of the rain makes sense to me. Sometimes, when it's not raining, I walk all the way home, rather than getting the Tube. Particularly at this time of year, when it is light in the evening.

It's only about two and a half miles, takes about forty-five minutes and makes me feel worthy. I can also get the 168 bus, although it doesn't go all the way, but I've never really got into travelling by bus. I think the tube is amazing and if I don't want to use it then I'll walk.

I am bothered by the lack of protocol about whether you are allowed to talk to strangers on a bus. On the Tube only strange people talk to you. On a bus many more people think it's socially acceptable to try and engage you in conversation. I don't think it is.

Nor is it socially acceptable to talk to you in the bus queue itself, yet that seemed to be compulsory for some people - another reason for tubing or walking. It had happened at the weekend. I was on my way back from south London – a tube wasteland, but a long walk – so I was waiting for a bus. A woman, maybe forty, started talking to me.

"Where have you been?" she asked.

"Just seeing some friends."

"Me too, where do your friends live?"

"Here," I say, suppressing the word "obviously".

"Mine too, maybe they know each other."

I am silent.

"I met an old school friend on the tube yesterday," she says.

I am silent again.

"Did you see the football? she asks.

"Which football?"

"When Argentina beat England."

61

"I'm Welsh," I say, instantly fearing a "me too".

Instead, I get, "At least you're not Argentinian."

Her bus comes.

We arrive at Chancery Lane, my cathode. Carefully, barge free, I leave the carriage and climb the escalator…

***

"Sandpiper, have you got 10 minutes?"

Dev wants to see everyone before they have their feedback session with the Managing Director. Since the feedback will be mainly based on Dev's appraisal of my performance, it makes sense for him to meet the team members first. Whether this avoids disagreements later or is just good process is not clear.

Our manager, Dev, only joined last year, from another firm. He's alright, knows his stuff and is fair, most of the time. He's married, to Preetha, and they have a child already even though they are both only twenty-eight. They live in Walthamstow, near the dog track. We all went there once. I had a few bets but didn't win. No one else won either but they seemed to enjoy it, nevertheless. I wanted to win. My parents used to do the pools every weekend. They never won. I never understood why they did them if they never won.

"Can I just get a coffee?" I ask.

"Sure, get me one too, I'll have a cappuccino thanks, see you in five."

There is a café in the basement of our office. It sells food and drink at subsidised prices. It isn't that much cheaper than outside but probably just enough to keep us in the office, which is presumably its aim. There is a free coffee machine on our floor but whatever comes out when you press 55 – apparently a freshly brewed coffee with milk - has clearly never seen a cow or a coffee bush (is it a bush, or a tree?). Again, presumably deliberate, so that you are encouraged to buy them downstairs.

There is also a gym downstairs, although I have never used it. I am not a big user of gyms. Alright, I have never been in one since I left school. I know that work gyms have exercise machines – not ropes and pommel horses and mats like a school gym – but I also know that everyone in there will be strong and fit and muscled and make me look inadequate. I am not embarrassed about my body but nor do I think of it as an asset.

I haven't really had any proper exercise since I left school. At university the group I hung out with weren't the sporty ones they were the cool, drinking ones, and once I came down to London there really wasn't the time. The firm supports various teams - five–a-side football, a rugby 15 and a rowing team – you have a chance to sign up at any time, but I have never done so. Two of my colleagues are in the rowing team and I can tell by looking at them, even in their suits, that I would be embarrassed standing next to them in the gym. Even before they row two kilometres in ten minutes, or whatever they do.

At my age, despite the lack of exercise and the smoking, I feel OK. I eat well, or often at least, don't drink alcohol every day and have been known to go for a walk in the countryside at the weekend once in a while.

One of my less healthy habits is my coffee consumption. I try not to smoke at work, even though it is allowed, as I know some of my colleagues and bosses don't like it, but all I do instead is substitute each missed cigarette with a coffee from the basement café.

This is my second of the day, with maybe four or five more to go, and Molly already knows what I want before I order. I just have to ask for the cappuccino for Dev.

"Not both for you, are they?" Molly laughs.

"No," I say. I'm not comfortable explaining that the

other one is for my boss, so I probably don't sound that convincing.

I have always had a problem with bosses – always is an interesting word when I have only been in a proper job for three years, but it had been the same in my later school years and at university. I want to be appreciated and recognised by them, but I do not want them to have that power over me. Surely I am a valid and valued person regardless of how they see me? My Dad says I need, and merit, more self-esteem.

I have some self-esteem, though, at least enough for this job. Here I am worrying about what Dev and the Managing Director will say and yet all I have to do is look stuff up and go to meetings. Imagine if I wasn't even really good at that.

When I first started as a lawyer I thought I would be in court all the time, suddenly announcing a new bit of convincing evidence that turned the jury round or saying, "My client won't live with that", in multimillion pound negotiations. Not that my law studies had suggested that – they taught me all about what constituted an enforceable cheque and how many years it took before you established the right to light for your property – but I had watched lots of movies with lawyers in who did that sort of stuff.

So, I spent my first year learning how to find books in the office library, photocopying and doing company searches – traipsing off to Companies House and getting a printout of the microfiche.

In my second year, I got to send other people to do the company searches and photocopying and spend time explaining what they have found in the library to more senior people. I don't yet get to explain it to clients although now I am a third year I do get to watch my seniors explain what I have explained to them to clients. Not always that well.

A couple of weeks ago, I attended my first "con' – conference with counsel – for a case I had been assigned to

64

work on – a chance to see what it is that barristers do.

The case is about a dispute over the building of a hotel, and whether our client was responsible for cost overruns, delays and loss of profits. There was a lot of money at stake so, Dev said, this one was almost inevitably going to end up in court. So, they would need a barrister to represent our client.

The process, which will be repeated many times in the future, is that we do all the hard work researching the case and writing it up. We then send the papers to the barrister. Then we go to see him (or her, although almost invariably him) – he never comes to you, even though his offices are always tiny and old fashioned - so he can tell your client whether or not they are going to win. They never say you won't win; they just give you a percentage chance. Presumably because if they say you won't win then there will be no court work and that's how they make their money. I couldn't tell from the con I sat in whether the barrister really thought that the client could win or was just ensuring appearance fees.

What was pretty clear, though, was that everybody – our Managing Director, the client people, Dev - thought the barrister was wise and important and that what he said counted. I had to make notes of the meeting so that we could send them to him for him to agree later.

"A latte and a cappuccino, Joe," says Molly.

"Thanks." I grab the coffees and go back to the lifts.

***

"Thanks for the coffee," says Dev, as I deposit it on his desk. "Take a seat."

We are in his office on the third floor. As well as getting to speak to our clients directly, promotion will eventually mean I will get an office of my own too.

"So how do you think your year has been?" he asks me.

65

I know the question is coming – that's how we do our appraisals – they ask me to tell them how I think I have done, rather than telling me what they think. Then I will get the answer they first thought of when I see the Managing Director later on today.

Last year I made the mistake of being honest and saying I found the work boring. Dev said he agreed that some of it was, but it was a good grounding for real challenge later and that they had to start everyone at a baseline until they knew their skillsets and abilities.

I wasn't going to fall for being honest this year.

"Tell them you have done really well and, if they push you, mention things that you could improve that are actually strengths." is what Stuart had said.

"Like what?"

"Like maybe you work too long hours or take on too many cases, so there are less to go around the rest of the team."

Good advice.

"I think I have had a strong year," I say

"I think so too," says Dev

"I think I did some good work on the Clark case and have been helping some of the first years get up to speed."

"I agree. Anything to change for next year?"

"Well, maybe I work too many hours and take on too many cases?"

"Really?" asks Dev.

"Well, you want to make sure all the team are getting a chance to contribute?"

"Yes… but we want our best like you to contribute more, don't we?"

"Yes, of course."

"And the more hours work, the more we bill, the more we can pay you."

"Of course."

66

"So, let's agree a target for next year. You did fifteen hundred billable hours this year, how about sixteen hundred next year?"

"Yes, sure, that sounds good."

So that went well! Could have been worse though, sounds like I am going to get a bonus and pay rise.

"Just one other thing."

"Yes?"

"Bill won't mention it."

"What?"

"Appearing smartly dressed."

How I dress? This is not going to be good, maybe I have spoken too soon.

"Is there a problem?"

"Not a problem but now you are out meeting clients then the firm does have a brand to maintain, you are an ambassador of that brand."

"And?"

"Maybe it's a one off but Bill said your shoes needed cleaning when he saw you at the con, and he asked whether you maybe need a new coat?"

To be fair, I am still wearing a coat I had bought at a market for £5, and I only clean my shoes on a Sunday night, but this is not good, being noticed for it.

"Thanks Dev, that's good advice; did William ask you to tell me."

"No, he just mentioned it to me, but I thought it would be better if you heard about it than not."

"I appreciate it."

"No problem."

"Will it impact my grading?"

"No that's already set, just a friendly suggestion really."

"Thanks."

"No problem. Can you ask Stuart to come in," Dev stands up.

Dev stands, so I do too.

"Yes. When will I see Bill?"

"I think he's planning to see you all before lunch. His secretary will call you."

"Thanks" I back out of his office, and into Stuart, who isn't waiting for an invite into Dev's office.

"Sorry." I return to my desk.

How I dress, how is that relevant? What do clean shoes say about your ability to get the job done? Maybe clients think they are relevant though? In that case, why hasn't someone told me about it before? So, the launderette, the supermarket and a new coat at the weekend! I am going to be busy.

***

"How was yours?" asks Stuart. We are sitting in the basement café, me with my third coffee of the day. He could only have been with Dev for a few minutes.

"Fine, yours?"

"Fine, I'm getting a bonus again."

"Me too."

"We should celebrate; you up for a beer or two tonight?"

"Yes, sure," although I am not sure I am. I need to go home and clean my shoes.

"I'll try and get Kev and Tasha along. It's a pity Liz is on holiday; she would have been up for it. Is there anyone else I should invite?'

"How about Tony? He's got his feedback today too."

"Yes, he'll probably want to go home, he's got a long commute, but why don't you ask him," he says.

I understand Stuart's reluctance about inviting Tony; he

68

does have a long commute, but he also has very little by way of a personality. He does not appear to be fully aware of that, though, so if he comes out for a drink, he will talk incessantly as if what he has to say is interesting. This self-belief is oppressive enough when he is sober. After a few drinks he thinks he is fascinating. Maybe I shouldn't invite him. No, that would be wrong and, anyway, with Stuart and Kev drooling over Tasha, and Elizabeth on holiday, who else am I going to talk to?

The way Stuart and Kev behave towards Tasha, and women in general, is really bad, in my view. One of my strong hopes is that I am really good in the political correctness area. I think I am politically correct, that I take people as people and neither judge them nor make assumptions about them. Of course, I know that I don't as much as I should, but I do try. And compared to most people, I think I am very good indeed.

No such self-control from Stuart or Kev nor, in my experience, many other supposedly mature and well-educated men. I've spoken to Laura about it a few times. She says it's not my battle. As long as I don't exhibit or encourage the behaviour, then I should leave young women to fight it. Fair enough. Certainly, when I tried to join the Feminist Society at university it was made clear to me that I was not wanted.

Laura also told me not confuse the risk of being considered sexist with being attracted to a woman and telling her. I imagine she knows that's not my problem with women, but it was sweet of her to suggest it is.

I lost my virginity when I was eighteen, which at the time seemed cool and not too late compared to my peers. Now, six years later, I think I have found it again.

***

"So, you'll invite Tony?" asks Stuart.

"Yes," I say.

"Why don't you invite Dawn too, I think she likes you."

"Who, the new receptionist? You're very funny."

"No, I think she does like you."

"Well, maybe I will then."

I won't.

***

We go on to a nightclub after the pub. It is Stuart's idea. He says he thinks he is going to cop off with Tasha, but she needs chaperoning a little bit longer before she succumbs. Kev, I am sure, has other ideas, as probably does Tasha. Lizzie told me a while back that Tasha has a long term very cool boyfriend she lives with.

I offer to get the first round in the club, leaving Tony to bore Dawn. She had come along in the end. I didn't invite her so I think Stuart must have suggested it to her.

Dawn and my opening conversation in the pub is about whether I fancy Lizzie and, if not, what is my type? Whether I was her type was surely more important though. Stuart had said that Dawn fancied me but beyond that opening gambit, there has not been any sign so far. Although she has happily agreed to come clubbing so that is a good sign? Maybe she just likes dancing, or she's Stuart's back up plan?

Tony has come clubbing too, although he lives miles away, so I am not sure how he is going to get home. Kev said maybe he thought he was going to get to stay at Dawn's –she lives round the corner from the office – but if I am going to struggle to do that surely Tony has no chance?

Neither Tony nor I enhance our chances by our topic of conversation. We are debating whether we are bothered about dying. Tasha had started us off by asking all of us to say

70

something that we were scared of. I think she means spiders or heights or getting a spot on your nose, but I say dying.

"There's no point in being scared of dying. It happens to everyone," says Tony. I clarify a little bit, that it is not dying but being dead that scares me.

"But you were dead before you were born," he says, "what's the difference?"

"Ah, but I didn't know I was dead then, now I know I will be."

"Sure, but once you are dead then you won't know again."

"Yes, but I know now that it will happen, and that the world will go on without me, that's far from great."

Anyway, the debate continues to the nightclub, so I think it wise to break it up by offering to go to the bar. I rarely find anyone who agrees with my view of existence, certainly among people of my age. I am happy to debate it with them but not too long. If I think about it too much, as I have a propensity to do, I can get really scared.

When I return with the drinks, Tony has gone – he said he had to catch his last train – ah well, one more drink, and maybe Dawn, for me, although not if I return to the mortality debate.

"Do you want to dance?"

"Sure."

We dance, and later, at hers, we fuck, and I get to try and get home at four in the morning.

"Are you really scared of dying?" she asks between bouts of sex.

"Yes, or of being dead, yes."

"I'm not, as long as it's not soon. When I am old, I will want to die. Being old won't be any fun."

Chernobyl explodes, Live Aid happens, Margaret

Thatcher wins again, and I get my own office.

8 September 1989

I have never been to a proper concert hall before. I have been to various gigs and church halls, but this is on a different scale. Apparently this is a really famous one, the Philharmonic in Berlin, home to the Berlin Philharmonic, one of the best orchestras in the world. Although, clearly not as good as the BBC Symphony Orchestra, if for no other reason than Laura is not a first violin in the Berlin Philharmonic.

Once our parents allowed me to, I stopped going to Laura's concerts. Laura said she didn't mind; she would stop coming to see me doing my homework. It was great to see her play, but she often appeared in concerts where you had to watch lots of other people's brothers and sisters also perform. Since the music they played (as well as the ability of some of the players) definitely wasn't my thing, the absence of a relative on stage made the Lauraless bits painful.

But I am here in Berlin, (a bit) more grown up and enthusiastic to see her perform as part of a world-class orchestra. She invited me a couple of months ago. Luckily I said yes, and the timing has enabled me to invite my newish "girlfriend", Suzanne, to a "cultural" weekend away, which I think is impressive, and hope Suzanne does.

We arrive that morning, check in at the hotel and spend the afternoon at the Berlin Wall. Now we are seated, looking forward to a wonderful concert, in this golden hall, with my golden sister on stage. We can see her from our seats in the stalls. She is a first violin. Not, though, the first violin. Laura had to explain that to me as I had been telling everyone my sister was the first violinist in the BBC Symphony Orchestra. One of my more educated friends had said that meant she was

72

the principal. I asked Laura and she explained there was the principal, then lots of first, and second, violins. Still, this was the BBCSO playing in Berlin, not too shabby for a Sandpiper, and, by the looks of it, for a woman. There were a few women in the violins, but the orchestra must have been 90% men, with the inevitable (according to Laura) male conductor in charge.

The Berlin Wall was weird. I have never been to a "real" monument before. It is covered in graffiti, with several memorials to people who have died trying to cross it. Of course, I know my history, and the wall has been there since I was born but it still seems an odd way to avoid the implosion of socialist ideas. If we can't explain and persuade people of the merits of equality and fairness (let's gloss over some of the other things in Soviet socialism), I am not sure we should suppress their ability to choose the other side. In that regard, I have always been a "bad", or ineffective, socialist.

Maybe there was, therefore, some irony in us coming to listen to a Russian symphony this evening, Rachmaninov's second. Although, according to the programme notes, Sergei had fled to the US following the Russian Revolution. I have heard of Rachmaninov (did he do that flight of the bee one? No that was Rimsky-Korsakov, close) but, given my limited classical music knowledge, I have no idea whether this is a good, or great, symphony. It's the BBC Symphony Orchestra, though, people are paying to watch, and Laura is involved, so they must be playing it well.

To be fair, it is an enjoyable experience, enhanced by the presences of Laura and Suzanne, I am sure, but I find myself wandering off a bit. We got up very early to catch our flight this morning, and it's now gone nine in the evening. I don't think I am going to fall asleep – that won't be good form – but my mind is wandering... or wondering...

Why don't the orchestra learn the piece off by heart? Why do they have all those pieces of paper to turn on their stands? Even I knew piano pieces by heart as a kid. I guess they were much shorter, and much easier.

If I lived in East Berlin, would I dare to try and cross the Wall?

How many people in East Berlin could afford the ticket prices for this concert, even if they were able to attend?

Will Suzanne let me sleep with her tonight?

Laura has never met one of my girlfriends before, although since Suzanne is only my third, she hasn't had a lot of chances. Will she like Suzanne?

Does that matter to me?

Will Suzanne like Laura? Most people seem to like Laura.

Being one of the violinists looks busy and involved, but some of the other players don't do much at all. Can I name all those blowy instruments, trumpet, trombone, French horn (why French?) but the wood ones?

How much of waste of time the guys at the back were, about ten of them just drumming one drum, each once, every ten or minutes or so, call yourselves drummers...

"Did you enjoy the performance? asks Laura.

I am not sure which of us she is asking, me, Suzanne, or her friend Zoe.

"I did," I say, "very much. And you looked like you did too."

"Oh, I love performing, the thrill of the greasepaint, the roar of crowd, the..."

"Polite applause and the occasional 'bravo'," says Zoe.

"Yes, to be fair a classical concert audience does not usually get as excitable and noisy as yours, but they do love the music and I love playing it."

Zoe, it turns out, is a "street performer", part music but also mime, and juggling. Quite versatile then. She seems a bit full of herself to me, but I guess if you are trying to elicit money in public, you have to be quite a confident individual. She and Laura had met in Venice, and she had come to see Laura play in Berlin and was going to try her hand at the square near the Wall for the week.

We are in a beautiful restaurant and I am here with three beautiful women. The early flight, interval and current drinks, and warm night conspire to distract me from their conversation.

It must be great to have people come to watch you, to hear you play, or sing, or act. Even if, in Zoe's case, she had to go to them. It must be great to have a talent, to be recognised, to be famous. Maybe to be a movie star. I knew I wouldn't have the nerve to get on stage, or a set and perform (even if I somehow developed a talent) but in my head I could. And, in my dreams I did.

My fantasies aren't restricted to ones where I am famous. Sometimes when I used to go shopping with Mum and Laura, I would pretend that they were famous. Not me, them. I would be their bodyguard. I would stand outside shops while they went in, trying to look threatening, and checking out the people as they passed me. I lacked a secret service earpiece but was very good at the owl-like scanning of the horizon. It gave me something to do while they spent their time shopping but there was more to it than that. It was "other". Other than just being a schoolboy out shopping with his mum and his sister. I was a secret agent. I was a rock star. I could walk on water, or fly, or be a better dancer, or write a best-selling novel. Harmless stuff, really.

Suzanne nudges me. I come back to the present.

"Bored?" she asks.

"No, just thinking about a work issue."

"What work do you do?" Zoe asks Suzanne.

"I'm a lawyer, like Joe, although not at the same firm. I specialise in family law, divorces and child custody and things like that."

"Much more worthy than my stuff." I add.

"Do you like classical music Suzanne?" asks Laura.

"Yes a lot. I played the clarinet in our school orchestra and am a regular at the Proms."

The waiter comes over, "Are you ready to order?" he asks. We obviously didn't look like locals. I had been hoping to show off my schoolboy German. Even the menu is in English, so I haven't been able to help the women read it either. Ach so...

***

Dinner had been lovely, and we are back at the hotel, in Suzanne's room.

"You didn't tell me your sister was gay," she says.

"She's not."

"Really?"

"She's had boyfriends."

"So what? I think she might be. Have you ever asked her?"

"Really, you think so?"

I pause.

"Do you think Zoe and she are in a relationship?"

"I think so, yes."

'I will ask her.'

"Tomorrow."

I did ask her, at breakfast. She is gay. It turned out she had already had more girlfriends than I had, even though she only started dating girls late. Mum and Dad know. I think it is cool.

I didn't get to sleep with Suzanne that night, or ever. I didn't think that was cool. Maybe Suzanne is gay too?

The Wall came down two months later, the end of the Cold war was declared, Aldi opened its first UK store and Margaret Thatcher stood down. My 30th birthday passes uneventfully.

Freddie Mercury dies, and, despite being Welsh, Neil Kinnock loses the election to John Major.

12 August 1992

After years of seeing each other most days at work, Lizzie finally succumbed, and I managed to lose my virginity again. We went on a few dates – the cinema, a meal, a Rick Astley gig - and then she invited me away for the weekend. It (the sex, but really the whole weekend) was amazing, and it was the first time I had woken up in the morning with a woman in my bed. Or a man, just to be clear. Although there was that time me and my friend got drunk at University, but that doesn't count. We did wake up together and were cuddling whomever we imagined each other to be but nothing else!

That first morning I couldn't stop cuddling Lizzie. I had been worried the night before that I wouldn't be able to deliver so I didn't drink much. I had also doubled up, with some earlier in the day self-delivered hand jobs just to make sure I could last long enough.

I thought we had been great together that weekend but soon after she suggested we give it a rest.

So, I went back to my teenage tactics, and wrote her a poem, "Her", in reply and left it on her desk at work. ("Her", "She", not a lot of thought goes into the title of my poem for the current girl of my dreams!)

Her

I never wished for this
I will never be the same
You gave me more than I deserved
I will never forget your name

It could have been no other way
I knew that form the start
But the memories of you
Lie heavy on my heart

No one ever touched me
The way you did inside
But now there is no more
And a part of me has died

And if there ever is another
I will still remember you
The times we had seem endless
While I know they were so few

I wanted to do so much for you
But could only see the end
And the last thing you gave me
Was a heart that will never mend

So now that it is over
And no one tells me why
There is no way to explain
I can only say goodbye.

It worked. Her reply was to leave me a note in my
pigeonhole telling me to come round to her flat that night. I

moved in a month later and stayed.

***

Lizzie is Spanish by background. Her parents met at a university in the UK, but both are from Spain. Jorge's family is from Murcia in the south, and Carmen's from Madrid. Holidays with her grandparents plus her parents' efforts at home mean Lizzie and her sister Carol can both speak Spanish fluently. I think that is really cool, as is that fact that both their grandfathers had fought in the Spanish Civil War and both on the right, i.e. left, side. It was one of the reasons they had been happy to see their children emigrate.

Other than my Dad's National Service, there is no known Sandpiper war record. And when it comes to linguistic skills, I did not stick at any languages, not even Welsh, which was compulsory to study to O level when I had been at a school. Although I can say,
'Llanfairpwllgwyngyllgogerychwyrndrobwllllantysiliogogogoch'
and sing a few songs.

Lizzie got a scholarship to a Catholic boarding school at eleven, which, she says, gave her a healthy disregard for religion (she was once given detention for fighting with a nun, Sister Siobhan) and, somehow, a great deal of self-confidence. I thought boarding school would give you all sorts of issues, it certainly would have done that for me. I am anxious enough without thinking my parents don't love me enough to even keep me at home.

Lizzie's parents seemed to love their kids. They were forever hugging Lizzie or Carol, or each other. Apparently, Jorge called Lizzie every day when she was at university. I called my parents once when I was at university, when I ran out of money.

Lizzie went to Bristol to study law, got a 2.1 and, it

79

seems to me, hundreds of friends, many of whom I later got to know. After law college in Chester, she joined Allens in the same intake as me. There were ten of us in the intake, seven men and Elizabeth, Natasha and Amy. Everyone noticed Elizabeth, but Stuart was the first one to make a move. I did not think of myself as a contender for those standards of women and was not too bothered, preferring to throw myself into being excellent and enthusiastic at work.

Even with that studied or feigned indifference, when she turned up to the firm Christmas party in a gold dress and thigh length boots, I did notice and wondered what it would be like if I had been in her league.

I don't think she was ever relegated, so I must have been promoted. What accounted for my promotion? I was never sure, but by 1992 I am Jorge and Carmen's favourite to be son-in-law and all is good with the world. Dad and Laura love Lizzie too. Mum thinks I have done very well for myself. Although she does, despite her feminism, occasionally mutter to me about the balance of power in the relationship.

"You need to make sure that you at least wear the trousers sometimes," she once said, half, but only half, in jest.

But I loved Lizzie's self-confidence and assertiveness. For me, being able to be with her, and be seen to be with her, was more than enough. When you love someone they are always right, right?

That self-confidence, or trouser wearing, manifested itself in the wedding proposal.

"I think we should get married," she announces on New Year's Eve in 1992.

"Don't I have to get your Dad's permission?" I ask

"It was his idea," she says, and kisses me.

I am not sure I ever officially said yes, but it is one of the happiest days of my life.

We get married in July, to coincide with Cuba's

carnival season. The wedding festivities start in the Catholic Church nearest her home. To be allowed to make use of their facilities, I have to undertake indoctrination (is that the technical term?) in the Catholic faith, study the rhythm method and agree, when it fails, to bring up our children as Catholics. The church bit is actually quite moving, and the food and drink and party bit of the wedding is fantastic, other than my dodgy groom's speech. I have written another poem, but this time I try to be funny. I am not. Lizzie looks amazing and even forgives me my speech quite quickly. I ask Laura to be my best "person" and her speech is funny, eloquent and just in the right taste. She and Lizzie really seem to like each other, which is great.

The flight to Havana is the day after the wedding so I do not have much time to fret about my first experience of flying. In the end it is not half as bad as I thought it might be. Although since I was fearing falling out of the sky, I am not sure what half that would be, maybe you crashed but lived?

Havana is spectacular, doubly so with the carnival processions and crowds. We stay for a week in a four-star hotel on the beach, posh enough to have its own tennis courts, spa and a zoo. I have stayed in a hotel before but never one like this, and never as a "married to Lizzie" man. I go round with a grin on my face for the entire fortnight. Lizzie occasionally asks me what is funny. She believes me when I say how happy I am and how much I love her. I am and I do. Later in our relationship, even though it remains true, she becomes a lot harder to convince.

We make good use of the tennis courts. I learn early on in our relationship that along with Lizzie's confidence comes a real competitive streak. She is not great at tennis, but I have to make sure she wins sometimes, without allowing her to realise that I am doing so. It is a thin line, one I stumble over many times, like many of the other lines in our relationship.

I also make good use of the spa. Lizzie says she does

81

not need to. She claims she is beautiful enough already which, to be fair, is true. I sign up for yoga, at which I prove poor, and several massages, which are a revelation to me. I have never had one before and loved the experience, despite my assumption that it would be a little bit creepy, allowing someone to touch you so much. Lizzie and I touch each other a lot on that holiday.

We do also spend some real quality time exploring Havana, watching, and joining in, the processions. Some of our friends had warned us about the poverty and, by implication, the crime in Cuba. They were all communists so, apparently, they would think nothing of mugging, or worse, a couple of Western tourists. We have no such experience. Yes, I imagine if you wander around as an arrogant ostentatious wealthy tourist then you might get robbed, no more, but we happily walk the streets late at night without a hint of risk.

We spend our second week on the north of the island, in a cluster of huts fifty yards from the beach, along with, it seems, a dozen other honeymoon, or pre-honeymoon, couples. Now I am in heaven. Lizzie, sand and sea, yellow and blue, and warm; not the Gower - brown, grey and cold. I still get my favourite sound, though, the pendulum of waves, tuning in to the rhythm of my heart. Or maybe my heart is doing the synchronising. I could stay here forever.

We do lots of other tourist things – a boat trip to the islands, snorkelling, swimming with dolphins, caving (not my favourite thing but I am not going to let my fears kick in on our honeymoon). Fresh fish barbecued on the beach, lying in each other's arms, consuming a fair amount of rum, and cigars. I take to cigars as a cigarette substitute. Lizzie joins in, although it is not her best look, cigar in her mouth, smoke making her eyes water.

16 September 1993

I am 32, and in heaven.

No sooner have we returned from Cuba than Lizzie says she wants children. Her sister, Carol, has two already, even though she is five years younger. I have not really thought about it before she mentions it. I have waited a long time to be with Lizzie. I am not sure that I want kids in the relationship (sweet though I am sure they are –and turn out to be) until I have really had my fill of being with just Lizzie.

She changed firms after we moved in together. Allens doesn't really approve of relationships among its staff, or certainly not proper ones between people of an equal age. It seems less concerned with the above/below stairs goings on of some of the partners and younger staff.

I offered to move but she said she would.

"I am not sure you would be able to get another job," she says, then laughs to indicate she is joking. She does not really enjoy the new firm, they are much more a city firm, all posh boys and Sloanes. Maternity leave will suit her.

So now I have to worry about whether we can have children - several of the couples we know have been trying for years. And if we can, will the child be born healthy?

She is pregnant within a few months. Getting pregnant is easy, being pregnant less so. She can't keep anything down and has to be hospitalised on a drip several times in the early months. Very sadly, we lose her first pregnancy. Lizzie is inconsolable for a while. She is usually the strong one in our relationship and I struggle. I throw myself into work and wait for her to recover. Carol and her parents, though, are amazing and help her do so.

We go for a bunch of tests before trying again. Apparently, her system is "a bit allergic" to mine so she has to be much more careful when pregnant, but so long as she carries them to term any child will be fine.

When she gets pregnant again, she takes early maternity and goes to stay with her parents. I accept this. While I feel a little bit usurped, as her carer, I want her to be OK more than I want to be the hero of the hour, or the nine months.

23 January 1995

"I want an epidural, now!" she shouts. I can tell she means it, not just because she is shouting, I can see she really is in pain and her eyes are tearing up. I want to help. I pop my head out of the door of the room, there is no one obviously medical visible. Not being sure that is the news she wants to hear, "They are on their way," I say. I hope they are.

There are lots of medical people when we arrive in the maternity wing, even though it is the middle of the night. Lizzie's waters break at home, but she patiently waits until she gets to two minutes between contractions. We have been packed for a week now, with the due date having arrived and gone and she is due in to be induced at the weekend. Spike (we know it is a boy but have not decided on the name) must have known the game was up and decided to arrive anyway. Starting to do so at 2 am, is of, course, one way of him announcing that our days of proper sleep are over.

Now, finally, "Term" is here, and "Spike" is ready. I am not sure Lizzie is. We had discussed pain relief and gas and air and epidurals at the NCT antenatal classes. Epidurals are safe but you can't have them too early because then they will wear off before the pain reaches its peak. You can't have them too late because then you won't be able to push.

The midwife appears

"Can she have the epidural please?" I ask.

"Hasn't the anaesthetist been?"

"No."

"I'll chase him up. How are you dear?"

"Fine."

"No, not you, your wife!"

Lizzie winces. "I think he was just trying to be funny. I am fine but please chase up the anaesthetist."

We have been playing classical music to Spike for a couple of months now – Laura had chosen the tracks for us - propping the tape machine on Lizzie's belly at night. I have brought it with us, and it is playing away in the corner of the room. "Morning Mood" starts (yes Laura, I know it is Ibsen), the sun is shining (we have been here for six hours so far), our child is on its way.

This is what I imagine men missed out on for so many centuries, as they left their wives to give birth alone. I am going to be different. I am going to add being a great father to my loving husband role. If I think about it, it is extraordinary: the "boy from the valleys" a husband, a father, with a proper job. My parents will be proud of me, I should be proud of myself. I will make sure "Spike" knows how much he is loved and spend the time with him and Lizzie. Nothing is more important than the two of them.

I look at Lizzie. She is lying on her side, facing me, while the anaesthetist inserts the epidural. I smile at her and she smiles back. I step to the side of her bed, hold her hand and kiss her on the forehead. She grabs my hand extremely tightly as the epidural goes in.

Now my eyes are watering.

30 September 1996

I attended the Labour Party Conference once, in Blackpool.

When I started at Allens they had discouraged my left-

85

wing stuff but once it looked like Labour might get elected they were delighted that I was a longstanding member and actually paid for my conference fee and hotel. It did make me feel like a bit of a spy, but I really saw it more as a chance to bring two organisations that I had real attachment to closer together.

Lizzie and Ian, only 18 months, came with me, and I would return to the hotel on the Blackpool seafront each night full of excitement at what I had heard.

Tony Blair was awesome.

"Friends, colleagues, this year we meet as the opposition. Next year, the British people permitting, an end to 18 years of Tories, we will meet as the new Labour government of Britain."

Even the more messianic stuff.

"At the time of the next election there will be just one thousand days until the new millennium, a thousand days to prepare for a thousand years."

And the stuff I believed passionately.

"We are not a sect or a cult. We are part of the broad movement of human progress, the marriage of ambition with justice, the constant striving of the human spirit to do better, to be better."

Blair talked about education. As new parents, as lawyers who believed in justice, as believers in equality (not a lot of that word in Blair's speech to be fair) shouldn't we do more? Hard when you have just had your first child and bought your first house.

Everyone at the conference seemed to be either a lot younger or a lot older than me, although I was only eight years younger than Tony Blair. Some of them definitely outdid even me for poor dress sense. But the weirdest bit of the conference was the evenings. Every day, after the main sessions, all sorts of splinter meetings went on. It was like being at the Edinburgh Fringe, most were attended by single figure audiences and had impenetrable content. There were a few corporate events where, like my firm, businesses had worked out that Labour might be in power next year. I went to a couple of Lawyers for Labour things, well attended and, with the Blairs' background, almost celebrity lawyer parties. I felt quite cool to be there and managed to shake Tony's hand at one.

Ten months later, Lizzie and I watched with much excitement as Blair won, and then with much disappointment six years later as he invaded Iraq. So much for the "broad movement of human progress".

Diana, Princess of Wales, dies, the Good Friday Agreement is signed, and Susie, our daughter, arrives.

14 May 1999

"So, what story do we want tonight? I ask.

As if I have no idea.

"Elvis and Presley," they shout together.

It is their favourite, even though they have heard so many of their stories before. I had started making up tales about these two monkeys a couple of years ago and now nothing else was as popular. In moments of excitement, I think I have a great children's book to write although I doubt whether Graceland Inc. will let me keep the monkeys' names. It would be so disappointing, for Ian and Susie at least, that I have never tried to write the book.

"Snore."

"Snore."

"Snore."

"Elvis," says Presley.

"Snore."

"Elvis!"

"What?"

"You're snoring really loudly!"

"No, I'm not." ..." Snore."

"Yes you are."

"I never snore, you know that."

"Whatever you say. Anyway, it's time to get up."

They get up and go down to the river for breakfast. They have bananas and coconuts and water from the river.

The sun is shining and reflecting golden in the river. It is a perfect day.

"Hello Elvis. Hello Presley."

It is their friends, Ian and Susie, coming down to the river to play.

"What shall we do today?" asks Ian.

"Let's play coco ball," says Susie.

"We'll need more than just the four of us."

So, they set off to see their other friends and get a bigger group together. They also collect two halves of coconut shell and tie them together with grass. They have a ball.

They have to pick teams —Elvis is one captain and Susie the other. Susie picks Presley and Ian and three others for her side. Susie goes in goal for her team and at half time they are leading three one, Ian having scored two of the goals.

In the second half, Elvis' team bring the score back to three all. Susie swaps with Presley in goal and, with two minutes to go (according to the position of the shadow of the big tree), Ian crosses the ball and Susie heads it past Andy, a big, but slow, monkey that Elvis had put in goal for his team.

4-3 to Susie and Ian and Presley's team!

They rest afterwards, while Elvis and Presley tell everyone stories of previous games that they had played in. And some they hadn't, as they make up ever more incredible events.

"Do you remember the time I went past three lions and

a rhino to score the winning goal? Asks Elvis.
Presley laughs, "I think it's time for bed."

I lift Ian gently out from under Susie's sheets and place him in his own. I kiss them both on the forehead and go back downstairs.

"Are they asleep?" Lizzie asks.

"Yes," I say, "they are asleep with Elvis and Presley."

"You should write that book you know."

"But what would I call the monkeys?

"Call them Ian and Susie, they would love that."

"Great idea."

She sits down, "What you are doing now?"

"I have some work to do," I grab my briefcase

"Can you just unload the dishwasher first?"

"Sure," I put my briefcase down again.

"How was your day?" I remember to ask.

"Fine. Yours."

"OK, although Derek doesn't want to pay us for the work on his property litigation. He thinks he should have won a lot more in damages than he did."

"Can he do that, refuse to pay?"

"No, because the court award includes our costs, so it's our money but he wants a recognition from us that we could have done better."

"Have I met Derek?"

"I don't think so."

"Who's the one whose wife ran off with the builder? She was called Annabel?"

"That's Mike, he was accused of insider dealing."

"I quite liked Annabel, but she didn't like me at all."

"I'm not sure that's true. Mike liked you so she wasn't so keen for us to come round too often."

"Will he go to jail"?

"It's always tough to get a jury to understand these cases so it could go either way."

"Do Mike and Annabel have any kids?"

"I don't know."

"That will be tough on the kids if they do, their mum runs off with another man and their dad goes to jail, presumably Annabel would then have to take the kids?"

"Yes, I'm surprised that she hasn't got them already, I thought women always got the kids."

"I think courts usually find that the Mum is a better permanent parent to the children, but Annabel didn't want them, I think she was having an early mid-life crisis.'

"Are you going to have an early mid-life crisis?" I ask

"Are you going to commit a crime and get yourself jailed?"

"No."

"Then I will stay with you, at least until Ian and Susie have left home."

"Thanks."

"Don't mention it. Are you going to unload the dishwasher?'

"Only if you give me a cuddle".

A new millennium, a new Dome in Greenwich, a new TV series - "Big Brother" - and an old favourite, England crashing out a of a summer football tournament early.

PART THREE - HEALTH AND HOPE

2001 to 2020

1 February 2001

I Google Health Anxiety.

It used to be called Hypochondria. That sounds much more medical, more real.

There are lots of websites, which help you self-diagnose Health Anxiety.

"Have you, during the past six months:

- Been preoccupied with having a serious illness because of symptoms?
- Felt distressed by this preoccupation?
- Found that this preoccupation impacts negatively on all areas of life, including family life, social life and work?
- Needed to carry out constant self-examination and self-diagnosis?
- Experienced disbelief over a diagnosis from a doctor?
- Felt unconvinced by your doctor's reassurances that you are fine?
- Constantly needed reassurance from doctors, family and friends that you are fine?
- Not really believed what you are being told?"

I score 100%, all of the above.
Why?

So, it's apparently caused by stress, or a recent illness or death in the family, or another family member may have worried about my health when I was young. I don't remember that happening.

Or I may be a 'worrier' (sounds like warrior if you say it quickly? That would be better). I might be a worrier generally. I might find it difficult to handle emotions and conflict, and tend to "catastrophise" when faced with problems in my life?

Now that is getting closer. But is that a proper illness, or just part of being sensitive and aware? Isn't it really just a matter of degree, how much you worry? How pathetic you are? So long as it doesn't stop you functioning it's OK but if it does, it's an illness?

I say pathetic; that's how I feel about myself. And it's reinforced by the way people talk about mental illness generally. Lots of people express sympathy for someone with cancer or a physical injury. Less so if someone just has something "in their head". Mental illness is not really respectable.

I hear people at work talk about it all the time (probably not really all the time but when you are paranoid...). How "so and so" is "a bit OCD", or "so and so has had to have time off for stress" or "Jenny never came back from maternity leave because she got post-natal depression".

Sadly, even I used to join in that game. I once told a joke at a works dinner (one of those events where everyone has to stand up and tell a joke):

Q. How many hypochondriacs does it take to change a light bulb?

A. An infinite number. One to change it and the rest to come back every day to check it's actually been changed.

Not that funny, and no-one laughed particularly

vigorously, but I got it, and no one objected to the implied criticism of its sufferers.

So, what can you do to cure it? I have tried. I joined an organisation called Anxiety UK, for £30 a year and got a subscription to Anxious Times (see what they did there!) and Headspace.

There are loads of self-help books. I have read two in the last few months:

- *Get out of Your Mind & into Your Life. The new Acceptance & Commitment Therapy.*
- *Reinventing your life. The Breakthrough Program to End Negative Behaviour... and Feel Great Again.*

They Like their Capital Letters. They basically tell me to think differently, to stop being pathetic, to get over, or used to, it. To Calm Down! Great! Or you can get some drugs or go to therapy.

12 August 2001

"Do you want a cup of tea?"

"Yes please. I would make it, but I think I just need to lie here. I think I had too much to drink last night. My head hurts."

I laugh, "You did have too much drink, and I had to put you to bed!"

"Dad, come in the pool," calls Susie.

"I will honey, I just need to make mum a cup of tea."

She had too much to drink last night, after we had put the kids to bed. Lizzie is always a pleasant drunk though, so it had actually been quite fun. And it doesn't happen very often either - mainly on holiday or at Christmas. I am drunk more often, and sometimes slightly less pleasantly than her.

Putting my paper down and getting off my sun bed, I go through the patio door into the kitchen. I have to take my glasses off; they are those ones, which react to the sun. They are great, except that they take several minutes for the darkness to fade when you go indoors.

We love this apartment. We bought a two-week summer timeshare last year. So, this is our second time here. We have eight more years after this if we want. My guess is that we will keep it. It is perfect for us

It wasn't that expensive either. Well, it was, but you can pay in instalments, so it is the same as buying a holiday every year. Flights used to be the most expensive bit of a foreign holiday, but it is amazing now how little it costs to fly with the new low-cost airlines. Yes, you have to be really organised to get the cheap flights, get up in the middle of the night to get to the airport, and fight to get seats together, usually squashed up in the back of a plane for two hours, but it makes the holiday affordable on my salary.

We flew out with Go, from Stansted. Lizzie's parents are coming out to join us on the same flight next weekend and then we are all flying back a week later.

Why have I started to think about going home already? Typical of me! We have been here three days, we're having a great time, and I am already planning the return to work!

Let's make that cup of tea and get in the pool.

It's not our pool, it is communal for the apartment block, but that is actually better. We already know several of the families who have the same timeshare period as we do and almost everyone who comes has young children.

Almost everyone who comes is British too. Before I ever went abroad on holiday, I had assumed that one of the exciting things would be the different culture and languages, which would enrich the experience. I do love it here but it's as Spanish as Center Parcs. They will even lose their local currency next year when everyone other than us moves to the Euro.

Not that there's anything wrong with Center Parcs, we have been there several times, and love it too, although Lizzie watching Ian being chased down the water chute by someone else's poo definitely dented our attachment to the place for a bit.

Last year here had been our first proper holiday for just the four of us. Prior to that we had always holidayed with the laws or in laws. None of them came over last year. It was also the first time Ian and Susie had been on a plane. They thought it was really cool. It was amazing really that they had flown that young. I hadn't been on a plane until my thirties. That was also the first time I got a passport. Five years after I got my driving licence. Lizzie has been flying since she was about ten and learnt to drive when she was seventeen. I learnt to drive when the firm finally gave me a company car.

My first passport had been for our honeymoon. It was amazing, probably the best two weeks of my life. In my head, I could honeymoon with Lizzie forever.

I look at her now. She's the most attractive forty something I have ever seen. I am not sure how I managed to end up with her. I have known her ever since I came to London to work but that was nearly 20 years ago, and we only started going out in 1992. She had lots of boyfriends before me. I had no proper girlfriends while I was in London, until her.

Although we only started going out in 1992, it moved quite quickly, and we actually got married a year later. And, since then, we have had Ian and Susie. If I could repeat the last ten years on a loop forever that would be fine by me.

When the kids are older I hope that they will think it is amusing rather than naff that they are named after my favourite singers. While they are still young, I have not explained to them how cool their names are. Lizzie hadn't wanted to, but on this she had let me have what I wanted. Or she quite liked the names anyway. I did have to compromise on Susie rather than Siouxsie and Lizzie drew the line about Curtis as a middle name for Ian, but even so I was delighted and, if it is possible, love them even more because of their names.

Lizzie loves this place and says I am a different person when I am here – I assume in a good way – more like the man she married, she says.

Ian and Susie love this place too. We can tell. They will spend the whole day in the pool if we let them and there are no demands for cartoons or food or for Ian to stop pulling Susie's hair. Am I romanticising this a bit? Probably, but it is amazing.

"Dad, come in the pool!"

"Sorry, Susie, let me just finish making mum's tea."

I fill the kettle and switch it on. Do I want one? Not tea, coffee. I try to cut down on my coffee drinking when I am on holiday, but it is noon, and I haven't had one yet so why not?

"What do we want to do for lunch, honey?"

"Nothing yet, they only ate breakfast at ten, so they won't be hungry for a while yet." OK, just a tea and a coffee then.

I give Lizzie her tea and drink half my coffee quickly. "Here I come,' I cry out to the kids.

I stand on the edge of the pool and dip my foot in the water. It is warm.

"You're not at the Gower now boyo."

Ian joins me at the side of the pool and I throw him in. Ian is laughing and he surfaces –strictly he does those things the other way round – and swims off. He is already a good swimmer. Susie is still a bit unsure in the water without her armbands, although we are working on it this holiday. She will be there soon. Swimming is one of the few areas where I am ahead of Lizzie. In most, to be fair, she is ahead. She had learnt to drive, fly (in a plane, not by herself, although she would be up for trying), and ski before I met her. I have never skied; why ruin a holiday by being cold and falling over a lot? –although Lizzie says she wants to take the kids when they are a bit older.

But I had learnt to swim really early. In fact, I can't remember when I couldn't swim, whereas she had not learnt until her teens. That was just weird to me, but I guess I grew up near the beach. Lizzie grew up near Heathrow, maybe in fact she could fly!

"Come on Susie," I urge, "Let's have a go at proper swimming, shall we?"

She paddles over and proffers her left arm. I let the armband down, swap arms and she is ready.

The shallow end of the pool is just about the right width for her to set off and still be above the surface by the time she gets to the far side. She climbs on my back and we set off for the shallow end. Ian doggy paddles alongside us. Lizzie waves at him and he tries to wave back, toppling to one side and under the water as he does. He grabs my leg and pulls himself back up. Both of them now on my back, I am going to sink. Carefully, because Susie doesn't have her arm bands, I start to sink to the bottom of the pool.

"Mum," cries Susie, "Dad's sinking."

"Well quick, you'd better swim to safety Susie, you too Ian," she says.

Requiring no further prompting they both set off and Susie paddles quickly after Ian.

I surface. "Susie, you're swimming, by yourself," I cry.

"Mum, I'm swimming by myself!'

"Wow!"

"Yes, I can see!'

"I'm swimming daddy, like Ian!

"You are!"

"Quickly though; last one to the end of the pool has to make lunch!"

That is going to be me. Maybe we will go out for lunch. I clamber out of the pool and pick Susie up, "Hey princess, now you're a mermaid, maybe your legs will turn into a fishtail."

"Maybe all of me will turn into a fish."

"We'll still love you... unless we run out of food and want some sushi," Lizzie laughs.

Lizzie has an odd sense of humour sometimes. She says she likes my sense of humour, when I bring it with me, but hers is different from mine – more odd, surreal. And she often amuses herself so much that she will burst into a fit of girlish giggles while we are all trying to work out what was funny about what she had said. I put Susie down.

"Do you guys want an ice lolly while I make lunch?"

"Yes."

"Yes."

"Lizzie?"

"No, but I'll have another cup of tea if you're in the kitchen."

"How's your head?"

"Better; one more cup of tea and a sandwich and I will be ready for a game of mini golf this afternoon."

In my view, a crude attempt to appeal to Ian and Susie. Even more so than my offer of a lolly. They both rush over and start cuddling her.

I retreat to the kitchen, put the kettle on and grab three lollies from the freezer. Ian will want lemon and Susie will want strawberry. I had better eat the blackcurrant one.

At least I would have done, if mine hadn't attracted one of Spain's large scary wasps. Now this is difficult. On my own I would have retreated indoors. If it was just Lizzie and I, she, knowing I don't like wasps, would have dealt with it. I can't have Ian and Susie either see or learn my phobia.

The trick, of course, is to have a cigarette with my blackcurrant lolly, thus driving the wasp to a less smoky zone, while neither smoking near the kids nor driving the wasp to them and their sugary treats.

But thankfully, before I have even lit up, it flies away to more productive mischief elsewhere.

One night during our honeymoon in Cuba, I was feeling tired, but Lizzie wanted to go out, so she went with another couple we had met in the same hotel. By the time she returned, I had hidden myself in the bathroom, being the only windowless room, while cockroaches and all sorts of other creatures –giant praying mantises, ants the size of donkeys, all of which seemed to be able to fly - threw themselves at the bathroom door to try and get me. Lizzie found me curled up in the bath, with, so she said, a large spider watching me from the ceiling.

I love "abroad" and want local language and culture and currency but nothing worse than British fauna is preferred - maybe some exotic butterflies and birds, but nothing scary or large or crawly.

They don't have that sort of stuff on the Gower.

The World Trade Centre collapses.

25 November 2002

"So, when did you decide to make an appointment to see me?"

"My doctor suggested it. I saw her a few weeks ago before I had to get on a plane to New York. I had spent the weekend before Googling... I was actually Yahooing. Apparently I am the only person in the world who still uses Yahoo and has a Blackberry... where was I? Yes, Yahooing Congestive Heart Failure and Flying."

"And what did Yahoo say?" he says, offering me a chair (not a couch I notice).

I sit.

"It's safe apparently, although you need to watch out for Deep Vein Thrombosis, take two doses of your medication with you, in case you lose one, and a note from your doctor, in case the crew need to intervene."

"Did you get a note?"

"I actually went to see her between the Yahooing and the flying. She told me I hadn't got Congestive Heart Failure, so I didn't need the medication, or a note, but I did need to Calm Down! She didn't use those exact words because, I guess, that would be undoctorly, but that was what she meant. She suggested I see you when I got back from New York."

"So, you have managed to make it safely back from New York?"

"Yes."

"And what does that tell you?" he smiles.

"You mean that she was right?"

"Was she?"

"Not necessarily; medically I might still have Congestive Heart Failure but got away with it. But I do think she was right about coming to see you."

He is starting to scribble some notes.

"So, is this the first time you have worried about your health?"

"Sadly not."

"When was that then?"

"The first time I remember was in Switzerland when I was eighteen. Is that too long ago?"

"No, go on."

"I had gone to Zurich over the summer to see a friend, as he was working at the university there. We had a great time although I do remember climbing the hills above the university

100

and suddenly coming upon a ledge and a massive, massive drop. I froze for what seemed like a long time and couldn't breathe properly for maybe an hour or so. I did not go up there again."

"You're not interested in my vertigo, are you?" I add

"Keep going."

"Anyway, I found a lump, on my chest, above the middle bit of your ribs – the sternum. Can you get a lump from fear of heights? I assumed not. According to my friend, it was a "fatty lump" – his elder sister had had one in her hand that had been cut out. According to me it was cancer and I needed to go home immediately to check it out. A fretful second half to the visit ensued before I saw my GP and had a minor operation (really more of the equivalent of having your nails cut) to remove the cyst. It was not cancer; it was a fatty lump."

He looks up from his notes. "What did you learn from that episode?"

"For me my fear was rational – I smoked – that gave you cancer – so I had got it. Why I thought my lungs were on the outside of my chest, rather than inside, is not clear to me now, but it certainly didn't seem to impact my thinking then."

"Do you still smoke?"

"Yes."

"Why?"

"Many people think that it's one of the odd things about me, given my health anxieties. That I smoke. I have tried to give up loads of times, but mainly when I think I have got something and then it's too late. I did give up for nine months once and put on loads of weight – thirteen kilos – the weight of a small child. I was up at nearly 100 kilos one Christmas and decided enough was enough, so I started again. It is, I admit, an odd weight control programme. But even when I have managed to stop since, at some point I realise that I am going to die even if I don't have another cigarette and then my will fails me."

"You are right, we are all going to die."

Helpful?

"Do you care about how you die?"

Really, this is how we are going to deal with it?

"Do you care about the quality of life, about what you can still do when you are sixty or seventy?"

I summon a response, "For now I would settle for reaching sixty or seventy."

"What happened after Switzerland? Do you want a coffee by the way?"

I nod and he pours one while I continue.

"After I had my fatty lump cut out I was fine and went back to being moody and cool rather than fearful. And I managed to stay that way most of the time for quite a while."

"Until?"

"I don't know, maybe five years ago?"

"What happened five years ago? Anything that triggered it?"

"Not that I can pinpoint. Nothing, like, big, like someone dying or something scary."

"Anything?"

"No, although with hindsight, I think I can pinpoint it timing wise to a night in January 1998. I had to give a big speech at a retirement dinner after work. It went well, but when I got home, I felt sort of weird. And, when I woke up in the morning, I noticed that my breasts were swollen. Yahoo said that was a sign of lung cancer."

"Was it?"

"A sign? Or lung cancer?"

"Either."

"I think it is a potential sign although there a lot of more obvious ones. I did have a chest x ray and they found nothing."

"Was that reassuring?"

"For a bit."

"Only for a bit? What has happened since then?"

"Loads of stuff."

"Tell me about it."

"It'll all sound mad." I protest.

"That's what I am here for. You came to see me to talk about it. So, talk about it."

So, do I just do this? Say this stuff out loud to him. Is that how it works?

So, I start.

"So, as I said, five years ago, having maybe had the occasional episode since Switzerland, it really started. Switzerland is twenty years ago though and all men have some form of health anxiety, so at first I thought nothing about it, and it's only with hindsight that I recognise that it started then."

'We'll come back to your view that all men have health anxiety but what happened?"

"The first new thing after my lung cancer false alarm that I remember was developing a burning sensation on my back. I went to the GP and he referred me to a dermatologist. She said that she could not see any worrying moles, and that they did not usually exhibit any sensation if they were a problem."

"OK. And?"

"Since then, I have had three testicular scans, a throat check-up, four moles removed – I was not convinced at the first session – a neurological exam, an MRI and another chest X ray. And, so far, they have not found anything. I have spent a lot of money though, and not been a great person when I have one of these episodes."

More notes, lots of them this time.

"How have you been during one of the episodes?"

"Moody, scared, drinking too much, not engaging with my family."

"Have you been able to function at work?"

"Yes, weirdly, work is distracting. I feel like I have to perform at work, even if I struggle outside."

"What work do you do?"

"I'm a lawyer, at a big firm in town."

"Do you work hard, how many hours, and weekends?"

"I work quite hard I guess, maybe 60 or 70 hours a week. Some weekends."

"Have you always worked those hours?"

"Most of the time."

"When was the last time you had a holiday?"

"At Easter this year."

"How was that?"

"I spent much of the time lying in the sun imagining symptoms, worrying I was ill."

"You say imagining symptoms. Were you imagining them?"

"I guess so. Sometimes telling myself I suffer from health anxiety helps to explain the symptoms, but then I end up rationalising the need for tests as it could be something real this time."

"Do you have anything you are specifically worried about at the moment?"

"I feel like I am losing weight."

"Are you?"

"Not according to my scales, but I have only been measuring my weight for the past couple of weeks."

"And what do you think the weight loss means?"

"Cancer, I guess."

He smiles.

"And are there any other explanations for weight loss?"

I see what they say about therapy. They just ask you endless questions until the hour is up.

It proves to be the case.

104

"I think we need to arrange for us to meet again, get Sue to put an hour in for next time. I think I can help you."

"Great, I will do that."

22 December 2003

Extract from Diary, `Christmas Holiday in Spain 2003

Monday 22 December

Up at 10ish, back sore, LHS of chest hurting, went shopping, collection of symptoms, feet hurt, calves, chest, feel I am using the wrong word occasionally, sat on sofa, gentle pain above right eye, eyesight might be distorted so that see less well out of right than left eye, seem to be producing excess saliva, often licking lips unconsciously, hands seem to shake when doing things, out for meal, two beers, seemed OKish, bed, Lizzie had a go, not discussing this with her so left it.

Tuesday 23 December

Woke up 9ish, strange jumbled up thoughts/tried and struggled to make sentences in my head, does that make sense? Masturbated, got up, back a bit sore LHS and goes down leg, feet a little bit sore, OK in the morning, to supermarket, walk in town, legs hurt, carried box (big but light), arms hurt, scared, home at 6.30, aspirin, moved a few things around, tired/dizzy, tea, one beer, read to Susie, neck hurt, sore back of head lower RHS (did L hit me?), reread some of this book, some stuff sounds familiar and recurrent over nearly two years, what's that, MS?, would MRI have checked for that? Bed at 12.

Wednesday 24 December

Up 11ish, LHS back sore, feet, when I get up front pads feel sore, like walked on a lot, pretty soon passes up my legs, like yesterday if I walk on my legs for a while they get tired, have to try a hiking holiday, if I'm still up to it, anyway see what happens today, went for a two hour walk up and down mountains with I and S, felt OK, pulse a bit racy, backs of legs stiff when finished but that felt normal, writing poor here but felt better, Christmas day tomorrow, hopefully not my last, bed at 1 am.

Christmas Day

Up, presents, breakfast, presents (L didn't like hers), lunch, few glasses of wine, pain in legs/feet, toes hurt, upper right thigh hurts now, toes "burning", like the sensation after I went to bed last night, burning sensation on the front of my lower legs, see how we go but back to concerned/alcohol related? Back sensations also returned for a bit, later on feet, legs still hurting, right shoulder ache, then, bizarrely, all my teeth hurt, bed 11.30.

Boxing Day

Up midday, feet sore, rear of backs of legs discomfort, eyes blurry, will I go blind as part of this, guess so, help me, another 2 hour hike up and down mountains, one beer eve, bed 1 am, hurt back rolling over.

Saturday 27 December

Up at about 10, I and S were both sick, went to shops in car, played crazy golf, Generally OK but feeling weak, spent time with S today, I want to see her grow up, what is this and how long have I got? Will need to wait until get back to UK to look into and find out, also not drinking to forget about it, is it getting worse or am I just able to dwell on it here, not sure, logic says (if it's something) then it's getting worse, again how long have I got, not forty years anyway, presumably not more than one, my right thumb joint hurts now, if I bend it I'm sat here at midnight with my legs aching, my thumb hurting, writing this and burning sensation in my back, watching some movie, and I'll be in a coma in six months, God help me, help, what do I do? Bed, sex (again), had a spasm, which moved my right leg while lying there, have been having these for a while, infrequent but noticeable.

Sunday 28 December

Woke up 11.30ish, up 12.30ish, my tactic of sleeping long in the hope that the symptoms might go away isn't working, the reality is my only real hope is that this is hypochondria, an odd hope, I guess I write it down so that it shouldn't come true, like telling someone I'm worried my plane will crash, not a good way of dealing with being ill or dealing with hypochondria, so what's my action plan?

- Another week in Spain coping
- Get my medical results
- Research possible causes via web
- See recommended doctor and discuss, explaining prior tests
- Think about getting GP records
- See therapist end of month unless found cause

Pitch and putt pm, OK, tea, 9ish feeling funny RH top of first knuckle on each finger and index finger hurt temporarily, what's that, its joint pain this evening, elbow again, ankle, knee, and bed 1ish.

Monday 29 December

Up noonish, same old same old, took S to tennis, two beers, out to collect pizza eve, right ankle went, hurt to walk, recovered, OK say overall, bed, movie until 12.30 am, pains in shoulder, thigh outside, toes RHS, all RHS, then nose felt funny, sleep.

Tuesday 30 December

Up 10.30, didn't want to get up, only symptom free when I'm asleep, reminded the minute I get up as the one constant is my feet hurt when first press on the floor, I have often been bad tempered on this holiday, is that part of it or just a reaction to thinking about it? Shit I'm scared, S to tennis, stops, out for dinner eve, pain, shakes, same as ever, have I got worse over this holiday? Not sure, fuck, what am I going to do if I am ill? I'll never cope, it's only "hoping" its hypochondria that's preventing a full scale breakdown, S had a night terror, That will be all the time once this is diagnosed, no, no, no, please, no, no, no... I won't be around when she has these attacks, shit I'm scared, I said that before, going to bed, not feeling good inside, and the front of my legs hurt and my neck RHS hurts and...

New Year's Eve

Up 11.30, L said the circles under my eyes had gone, shop, cigarette, lunch, tennis with L, I and S (not vigorous), arms hurt afterwards, out eve for dinner, four hours, several glasses of wine.

My 2004 resolution; try and be around in 2014.

6 May 2005

I am ill at the moment, or at least I feel ill. Can you make yourself ill worrying about it? I hope that's what it is.

I could look the symptoms up on the internet but that doesn't work either. If you go on one of those health websites and type in headache or numbness in your fingers, they will tell you have Multiple Sclerosis or a brain tumour or something really scary like Creutzfeldt-Jakob Disease.

I stopped eating beef for a year after that got announced. Then they told us it could be dormant from the beef you ate in your childhood.

So, what are the symptoms of Creutzfeldt-Jakob Disease – loss of memory, loss of balance, shakiness – I have all of those.

Some illnesses aren't as bad as others –maybe if I have a long-term deteriorating illness then it won't be as bad as a terminal one? I really don't want lung cancer, not just because it will kill me but because it would be embarrassing as it would be self-inflicted.

I went for a run last week just to see whether I could, or whether I would keel over with a heart attack. I didn't. That's checking really, and you shouldn't do that. The more appointments and tests you have the worse it gets. You just need to get through it and, if it turns out that you are ill this time, so be it.

How does that help?

One of my friends is ill. He has had cancer for three years now. I struggle to understand how he is dealing with it. One of my wife's friends died of cancer five year ago. So, it

109

does happen.

Why not to me?

Sometimes, when I read the paper, I look at the obituaries and negotiate with God. I offer him (her?) a swap. He has to guarantee that I will live until the same age as the average of the deceased people. In return I get the certainty of living until then, but I have to agree to accept the offer before I look at the obituary page. There was a 93-year-old musician last week, that was good, then some politician who died at 55, not so good. I am not sure that God has entered into these negotiations yet.

Sometimes, when I am approaching a traffic light, again, I agree (with God?) that if it stays green I am not ill, but if it goes red before I get there I am in trouble. I am not allowed to speed up before the light, it has to just be fate.

Am I superstitious? I used to be, counting magpies, avoiding ladders, something –what? - with black cats.

I have started telling Lizzie what I am worrying about or writing notes to be found "in the event of my death". If I say I think I am going to die on this trip or not last through the night, it would be so weird if I foretold my own dëath that it must make it less likely to happen.

I try to be careful not to scare the kids, although I do occasionally send them random 'Just so you know I will love you always' texts, as if I have found myself on a hijacked plane or a runaway train.

Where does all this come from? My parents are still alive. I can't think of a funeral I have been to since Peter's. It's not as if I was ill as a child.

I had asthma (and took up smoking, really?) and one of my first exposures to a medical product was my trusty Ventolin inhaler. I don't remember much by way of medical intervention other than that.

Apparently, (I don't remember) my Dad shut my thumb

in the car door when I was four - presumably accidentally – and it had to be drained with a huge needle.

Later on, in my youth, I remember leaping from our climbing frame in the garden, targeting one of the 'Native Americans' surrounding our fort, but actually landing with my front teeth stuck into my right knee. It was plastered, rather than stitched, went septic, and ballooned up. I spent a month sat in my garden, looking like a very early-stage yellowish one-legged Michelin Man, and had to wear a brace for several years to push my teeth back.

I also twisted my knees several times playing football, my hand playing rugby, but I never broke anything else or spent a night in hospital, so far as I remember. Nor, as child/teenager, do I remember worrying about my health although I did spend a bit too much time mulling over death and dying - although at the time I would have said I was being moody and cool and dark, not storing up troubles for later life.

One of my teenage poetry efforts – titled 'Flame', opens with:

The pain will never end
In the death cell of my mind
The tears you cannot see
Will forever soak my heart.

That's what my worst health anxiety moments can feel like – being in a death cell, awaiting the end, a last meal, maybe a last night's sleep but it's all to be over soon.

Is this really how to analyse yourself, trying to explain it via a poem you wrote as an 18-year-old?

Maybe I do need to get a deeper understanding of how I feel and how to cope with it. But how much of this should I say to the therapy guy? I know he said he is there to hear mad stuff, but I don't want him to think I am pathetic.

111

Nor do I want him to think I am really mad and want to put me on tablets or send me on courses. I am, at worst, functioning, aren't I, and I don't think I am ill all the time.

Bombings on the London tube, Tony Blair stands down, Madeleine McCann disappears, the iPhone is launched, and I don't die.

8 March 2008

I have now been seeing Doctor West for six years. A routine has been established. He is trying to break it today by bringing along a couple of colleagues to discuss my "views on death".

"So, this is Trevor, and this is Janet. As we agreed at the last session I have told them a little bit about you, and we thought all four of us could have a chat today."

They nod and smile at me.

"Good morning. Of course, happy to." I say (am I?).

"So where should we start?"

"Why don't I get straight to the point we were discussing last time?"

"Of course."

This part is well rehearsed by now.

"I suffer from what you would all define as health anxiety. You argue that it is irrational as the illness is imagined not real. I think what I am actually anxious about is death. That anxiety is rational as it will happen?"

"So, all anxiety is rational if it is about something that will happen?"

"Not productive, but rational yes."

"So, it is rational to be scared of spiders, because they exist?"

"No, it's not rational to be scared of the existence of

112

spiders. That can't do you any harm. It is rational to be scared of them biting you or laying eggs in your brain (I read about it once, what can I say?) as there is a real risk of those things happening."

"So, it's like a fear of dogs. Of those that might well bite you, it makes sense. Or vertigo, if you could really fall it's rational, if no, then not?" asks Janet, still smiling.

"Exactly."

"So, do you have any irrational anxieties?"

"Yes."

"Like?"

"Like now. I am feeling anxious about this discussion and what you might say, or think, about me."

"Why? How could that harm you?"

"It can't really, which is why I accept it's irrational, but it still feels real."

It does, what have I got myself into? And I am paying for the privilege, probably more than usual as there are three of them!

"So, you would feel better if you weren't worrying about what we think of you?"

"Yes."

"Because the anxiety isn't helping you avoid any harm."

"It's just stressing me, for no purpose."

"So, turn that thinking onto your anxiety about death. Without trying to sound ironic, what harm is death going to do you?"

"It's going to mean I cease to exist."

"And that is a harm?"

"Yes, I think so."

"Well, some would argue that it's the opposite. The absence of harm, no pain, suffering, no feeling stressed?"

"No, that's not right."

113

"So, what's the harm that death brings?"

"Oblivion."

Here goes my central argument, let's see how it goes.

"You will presumably argue that oblivion, ceasing to exist, is not a harm. It's not a broken leg – that hurts. Oblivion doesn't hurt when it has happened. It is only the thought of it that hurts now. And worrying about it won't avoid it so it's unproductive to worry, i.e., irrational."

"Something like that, yes," says Trevor.

"Well to my mind it depends upon your view of what we are here for. Unless you subscribe to an afterlife then we are either random time-limited chemical reactions or we are something more."

"If we are just the chemistry then why even debate whether anxieties are merited or not, productive or not, they just are what they are. At this particular point of time in the evolution of the universe, atoms number one hundred billion and seventy-four through one hundred and two billion and ninety-seven - me – are just doing this thing and in less than a hundred years they will be part of a tree or several trees or broken down and reformed into someone else or a comet or another planet."

(How many atoms are we actually – I looked it up afterwards, and was out by masses, roughly 70 billion, billion, billion apparently.)

"Darkly put but yes, that's one version of the science."

"So those atoms don't 'care' what happens to them. They don't have a preference for being hosted by an anxious or calm individual. So, all that we have discussed would be irrelevant on that analysis."

"I'm not sure we would all agree," says Doctor West "but tell us about the 'something more' you refer to."

"I am not sure what I would call it and I am not precious enough to claim that I have any new view or argument. But there is something else – life, or a life force, something generated by the evolution of the configuration of my atoms such that 'I 'exist. I know I do, because I think I do, or whatever it is that Descartes said."

"So then, me existing is a thing, and from my point of view, a good thing, I have purpose and anything which seeks to prevent or undermine that is bad, or a harm. And it is reasonable for me to try and stop anything that undermines it, and it is reasonable for me to worry about the harm."

"But you can't stop it."

"I know but my feeling about it is genuinely well based and very different from a worm fearing its nonexistence in the beak of a bird, even though it can't prevent it either, not for long anyway."

"So?"

"So, when you all describe my health, or as we have established death or oblivion, anxiety as irrational. When you try to cure it that is really just your own anxieties wanting to suppress mine. You don't want to think about it so I mustn't."

I am definitely sounding paranoid, but I can't stop now.

"I often wonder why more people don't, or don't seem to, worry about it. I think it's because it doesn't help so they are rendered helpless – you are catastrophising, but because there is an impending real catastrophe, not an imagined one. And what would happen if we all thought things were hopeless – it would be chaos. So somewhere no doubt there is a government file – not one that will ever be released –which tells the government of the day not to let this form of Rational Helplessness ever take hold."

"You don't really think there is such a file, do you?"

"No, I don't, but I do sometimes wonder what would happen if more people thought like me."

"What do you think would happen?"

"I think, if we got past the chaos phase, people would

115

try and make the most of what life they had."

"Isn't that where people are already?"

"I'm not yet."

"So, let's work on that. In your next session"

"OK."

4 June 2010

I get into regular debates with my work colleagues about politics. They always start with the argument about how socialism takes away the incentive for people to be successful and therefore means the economy would be less productive overall, or those people will leave. I always win (happy to expand upon how) but then they move on to baiting me about my personal politics. If I believe that why had I gone to university, why was I a private lawyer, why did I not pay back all my income in taxes and volunteer in a night shelter?

All good questions, if I thought about it too hard, but not ones to be accepted when up against people who do not even BELIEVE, let alone act, on the principles I know to be right.

Allens introduced a Diversity Policy in 2010 – everyone went on a "gender and other differences are not an excuse for prejudice" course and the firm launched various networks. I wanted to join them all to show my political correctness but was not allowed to join the Women's or BAME (Black and Minority Ethnic) groups. I did become a LGBT Ally and dabbled with forming a "Celts are people too" group.

I was a wholehearted supporter of the initiative but couldn't help feeling that it was all a bit middle class, much like me and my colleagues. Are the real issues in society and the world going to be addressed by making sure there is a woman on each public company board?

I feel similarly about the whole climate change thing.

Will the planet avoid overheating if I separate my waste into different bags? It seems unlikely. I feel that my analysis is better than the analysis of people who genuinely (or so it appeared) believe these things will make a difference. Although, of course, both of us are much better people than those who don't even want to save women or the Maldives.

Where I fall down, though, or not so much fall down as, I reluctantly know, become irrelevant, is that I do not do what my analysis demands to really change things.

This is my continuing frustration with politicians, and Labour in particular. They do not deliver what their and my socialism demands. I guess the Labour Party, at least, has the excuse of needing be palatable enough to be elected. What's my excuse?

Some of my fellow lawyers do pro bono work for deserving causes or volunteer their service for benefits claimants or immigration appeals. I don't even do that. With the same impeccable logic, neither of those things will address the terrible economic or racial inequalities that exist so what is the point?

My dad hadn't thought this way, or certainly hadn't acted like he did. He had strived to do the right and best thing he could throughout his life. Maybe not for Laura, Mum and me, but for society. He had been a social worker, working with troubled teenagers in South Wales. He spent hours away trying to help in difficult situations or speaking at conferences about self-harm or gangs, or anorexia or teen suicide.

Dad started out on that career in Bedfordshire, and we had moved to Wales when he had taken a more senior position based in Bridgend. Mum was a science researcher (she claimed to have invented Fairy Liquid, but we seemed to get no royalties from the sales, so I guess she didn't). So, Mum and Dad invented things or helped people. Laura makes amazing music, and I check the clauses on office lease contracts. I make more money than the rest of my family though, and that is good, isn't it?

You didn't make much money as a social worker or research technician in South Wales in the 1960s, or the 1970s, or probably ever. My life wasn't as working class or poverty stricken as I would have people believe but there was not a lot of money around and I had to earn any spending money I wanted from an early age, especially as Laura's music tuition cost what little excess money our parents had.

22 September 2011

Laura performed in many, but I have never been to the Proms. But I have been to the Royal Albert Hall. To watch Adele sing.

Lizzie got the tickets for my 50th birthday. By that age you need taking out of yourself. The children, the career and your life are starting to evaporate.

Lizzie took me out of myself, thanks to Adele.

Lizzie is really, really good at present getting (and much else, have I said?). She always finds something I didn't realise I wanted but definitely do once I open it. She is harder to choose for, or I am less good at choosing what she wants. Spotting the thing she doesn't realise she wants is way beyond me. It requires a high level of empathy, apparently. I quite quickly got into the habit of accompanying my present with the relevant receipt so that she could exchange it for something she actually wanted. She was more, although not perfectly, forgiving with Ian and Susie and they had also worked out that if they wrote a loving message on the card then the gift became pretty superfluous. Not so for me, I had used up my reservoirs of poetry appreciation to win her in the first place, now she wanted something more tangible and thoughtful.

More thoughtful than a heartfelt poem? Is that

possible?

I did occasionally test that. For Christmas in 2010, I framed a picture of her at our wedding as background to a poem. The poem took many weeks to write, and she loved it.

Piano tunes and poems

If we met again, would we feel the same?
I know that I would

Let's go and play at snowballs
Let's get married in July, and call our first-born Spike
In your thigh length boots, you had me at hello
As they say in the movies

Latin cool, nobody's fool, with that funny middle name
Gone with the Wind, Conan the Barbarian, big men
How could I compete with them?
With piano tunes and poems, I guess
And maybe Acker Bilk?

I am no Wordsworth nor Byron
No Allende nor Garcia Marquez
I am Tiny, the awkward Welsh boy (o?)
Asking the woman for her love

If we met again, would we feel the same?
I know that I would

Three little words, they are not enough
But I can never say them too much
I love you, and always will
Mother of our children, lover in my soul

When I die, think only this of me
That there is a place in my heart, which you filled
We have had our ups and downs, our smiles and frowns
But the constancy of you carries me when I am weak

Footsteps in the sand
Like your dad used to say

That would only work once though so, as with the gift of the Adele tickets for me, events were sometimes a lower risk territory than the high-risk bag or jewels. Not for Lizzie either the cop out of a must-read book and she had no interest in modern music. I had done well with the Wimbledon tickets, and Kenwood, less well with Snow Patrol at the Roundhouse, which she, fairly, suggested was self-gifting masquerading as thoughtfulness. Great gig though.

Not as great as Adele in Kensington though. Ian had bought me her album, 21, wow to be 21 again… and I loved it. Admittedly though, album titles based upon your age seems somewhat lazy. Maybe Adele thought the music was good enough in its own right. By the same logic, Cosmopolitan's tentative, but unpublished, album title of 'Shipbuilding with Nero' indicates a certain lack of confidence in our music standing by itself.

Usually, I try to be slightly more obscure than Adele in my musical, and other tastes. Not for me the prosaism (is that a word?) of Downton Abbey, or supporting Arsenal, or Coldplay. I clearly liked Adele's music enough to be found shallow this once. Normally it would be Gavin and Stacey, Watford and Bon Iver. Not classy (although I think so), but not so mass.

Lizzie loved the Adele gig too and we had one of those (rarer and rarer) evenings of mutual shared pleasure. We sang along, we danced, we cheered, and we wanted it never to end. I didn't drink much. We had sex when we got home. Ah, to be 21

120

again, again.

11 April 2012

Friends and Family
Please join us on Wednesday 11 April 2012
At 2.00 pm
Finchley Memorial Crematorium
To celebrate the life of Catherine Myriam Sandpiper
(nee Jones)
And afterwards at The Grange

Laura touches me on the shoulder.
"Are you OK?"
I look up.
People are waiting.
Lizzie smiles at me.
"Mum died nearly two weeks ago. She and I had 50 years – not enough - together. And I miss her. We all do I am sure." I read, flatly.
I need to do better.
"I was saying to Laura yesterday, how weird it has been that the sun was shining on the day she died and has ever since. Surely we should have rain and storms and howling winds and clashing clouds?"
"I have decided it is a clue that we should talk about sunshine – about the sunshine in Mum's life and the sunshine she brought to the lives of others."
"One of the rays of sunshine in Mum's life was her grandchildren. Mum had two grandchildren, here today, Susie and Ian. She loved them, and they loved her. Mum was really proud of her grandchildren, so am I."
"Another ray of sunshine in her life was her friends. Many of you are here today and many of her favourite

memories were of her and Dad's travels all over the world with some of you. Barbara and Denis, Margaret, Pat and Frank. She got to the US, South Africa, Australia, New Zealand, most of Europe. Not bad for a girl from Cardiff. Thank you all for coming."

"She also put sunshine back, whether it was working in the local Citizens Advice Bureau or helping with the OAP festival or community hall or mentoring local sixth form girls. Mum was a feminist before it was trendy. She campaigned for equal pay for women at work and actively campaigned for more women in science and medical roles."

"Apart from Laura and me, the person who benefitted most from Mum's sunshine was Dad. They were married for over fifty years and he will probably miss her the most. You still can't believe she is gone, can you Dad. You always used to sing "you are my sunshine" to her. You were right."

Dad smiles at me, weakly. I smile weakly back.

"I know this is a humanist funeral, because that is what Mum asked for. She did not believe in a god. But maybe she was wrong, and she is now sitting on a cloud, with a mug of tea, reading her Agatha Christie? Hi, Mum, we love you."

"Just one more thing. I have lost one of the most important women in my life but there are two more. Lizzie, you have been amazing over the past two weeks. Thank you. And Laura, I have been rubbish since Mum died and you have not only dealt with your own feelings but also organised everything and got us focused on what she wanted and how to celebrate her life. Thank you sis."

"Thanks Joe," says Laura, and squeezes my arm.

I pick up my piece of paper and return to my front row seat.

The sun shines stubbornly through the windows of the crematorium.

***

I last saw Mum two days before she died. Dad and she came round for Sunday lunch. Ian, Laura and Zoe were there too. Susie had a party to go to. It had been a nice afternoon and Mum had seemed better than usual, although still pretty unwell. They had moved to London to be nearer to us a couple of years ago. Mum didn't like it. Dad threw himself into the local community activities, although that was easier if you were properly mobile.

Mum had a serious stroke five years ago and has never properly recovered. We thought it was awesome that she was still going but Mum was not good at being ill. Which of us is? But Mum really didn't like it and struggled to do the stoic thing of suffering in silence.

I got them both in the car, Mum in the front.

"Nice to see everyone," says Dad, "thanks for having us over."

"It was nice wasn't it Catherine."

"I'm not sure I want to go on," she says.

"Why not?"

"What is there to live for?"

"Catherine!"

Dad used to have this debate with her, but he had conceded defeat and just listened. I still engage.

"Well, there's me and Dad and Laura, and your grandchildren, don't you want to see them grow up?"

"Susie couldn't even be bothered to be there today."

"She had a party to go to."

Mum was the last of her family, both of her sisters had died several years before. I think she missed them. And she hated being ill.

***

123

Dad called me two days later.

"I am at the hospital; your Mum had another stroke and she's in intensive care."

He had tried to rouse her that morning, realised something was wrong and called an ambulance. It took twenty minutes to arrive.

"Why didn't you call me or Laura while you were waiting Dad?"

"There was nothing you could have done."

"Yes but you were on your own. We could have been at the hospital earlier."

Laura was already at the hospital when I got there.

"Where's Dad?"

"In with Mum, they are only allowing one of us in at a time."

"How is she?"

"Not good."

"How's Dad?"

"If she dies, he's going to be devastated."

"So, let's hope she doesn't die then."

A woman in a white coat emerges from the ICU.

"Are you Catherine's children?" she asks.

"Yes."

"Why don't you come through?"

"But I thought it was only one at a time?"

"I think you should come and be with your Dad, and Mother."

Mum never regains consciousness, although Dad thinks she knows what he is saying, or at least that we are there. We sit beside her bed for maybe half an hour. At some point in that 30 minutes, she dies. My mum, the inventor of Fairy Liquid, is no more. She is only 83, nothing in the great scheme of things. I kiss her on the cheek, again, and leave the ICU. I go outside. The sun is shining, and people are going about their normal everyday business, but my Mum and my Dad's wife has died, how can they?

Susie is really upset that she hadn't seen Grandma/Mum the weekend before she died. She wrote a note that we put in the coffin.

Grandma

Sorry I went to Eleanor's party. I wanted to see you, but I wanted to see my friends too. Mum said you understood and wanted me to be happy. How can I be happy without you?

No one said that people could leave me. I knew that rabbits could die, mine did, but not grandmas. Who is going to give me those cuddles now? Who is going to love me so much that your arms don't stretch far enough?

Who is going to teach me more Welsh? Rydyw'n hoffi coffi is my favourite sentence ever.

I hope heaven is a nice place. Dad said that's where you've gone but that I can't visit. I can speak to you though.

Susie XXXX

"I am so sorry for your loss," says the celebrant (that's what they are called at a humanist funeral).

"Thank you. And thank you for the kind words during the service."

***

Barber's Adagio for Strings – recorded by the London Philharmonic, when Laura had been a Second Violin – is playing in the background.

It is usually one of my favourite pieces of music, up there with things like She's Lost Control, Jailbreak or Hong Kong Garden. I am more aware of classical music than most because I have been to so many of Laura's concerts, but I still struggle to enjoy most of it, unlike the modern stuff I am into.

Not so modern, of course. Ian and Susie seem to be into all sorts of rap and house and electro - whatever those are- although they do approve of my love of Adele. Apparently she is quite a good singer/songwriter.

In reality the classical stuff I enjoy is usually because I associate it with something else, like a movie. Laura knows it and it really annoys her that I can't get my head around some really cool John Wilson piece but am a sucker for the Lord of the Rings theme tune.

So, inevitably, I did not fall in love with Barber's Adagio for Strings at a concert but when I watched Platoon, with it as the backing music. So, when I hear it, I see dust and Vietnam and body bags.

Everyone I know has a top ten music and a top ten movies list.

Mine are (not necessarily always in this order, it depends):

- Joy Division
- David Bowie
- Thin Lizzy
- Siouxsie and the Banshees
- Bon Iver
- Adele
- Snow Patrol (see, another modern one)
- The Jam
- Swell Maps (who?)
- Nick Cave.

I am not sure what Lizzie's full list would be, but it

would definitely include Santana, Earth Wind and Fire, Barry White and the Osmonds. She is a huge fan of Rick Astley.

I know her movie list better, as I have sat through all of them several times.

- Gone with the Wind (isn't it racist really?)
- When Harry Met Sally
- Whatever Happened to Baby Jane
- Bridget Jones
- North by Northwest
- The Way we Were
- Doctor Zhivago
- Any Woody Allen movie (until he got into trouble)
- Sunset Boulevard
- Now Voyager

My movie list is somewhat less impressive, at least to the Oscar committee, but I love them, nevertheless.

- The aforementioned Platoon
- Aliens
- Con Air
- The Mission (that has a really cool musical score, and some spectacular waterfalls)
- The Untouchables
- Gladiator, and almost anything else by Ridley Scott,
- Love Actually (I know but it is the closest I get to

Lizzie's list)

- Bladerunner
- Tarkovsky's original Solaris (my pre-prepared pretentious answer when talking to film buffs)
- The Lethal Weapon series.

The clear, on the face of it, boy/girl split on our music and movies does disappoint me, at least from a political correctness point of view, and I have tried studiously not to segregate the cultural influences on Ian and Susie. Or is it 'Susie and Ian'? Why do I always describe the two of them that way round? What unconscious sexism is creeping in even to how I introduce my (there I am at it again), our kids? Despite my/our efforts, they are both repeating the gender divides of their parents.

***

The celebrant is looking at me quizzically.

The service is over and everyone else has gathered outside.

"Will you come back with us to the hotel? You are more than welcome," I say

"No thanks," she says, "I have another service in an hour."

Life, or death, moves on.

Laura and Zoe organise everyone back at the hotel, getting the guests to sign the remembrance book, making sure everyone has enough food and drink. Making sure Dad is not left alone. He is sat with Lizzie and the kids, nursing a pint. Lizzie has been amazing for the past two weeks, she has been really supportive, and said what a good son I had been.

I have, I think. Not a great one but I always loved my Mum, and I had given her grandchildren and got a good job. Laura spent more time recently with Mum and Dad, even when they had moved to London, but I saw them most weekends. We took them on holiday, to Spain, to Paris. We had even had a nostalgia trip to the Gower, staying in the same old caravan site and playing Ludo while the horizontal rain lashed the caravan windows. We also had a family holiday at Center Parcs with Lizzie's and my parents.

Lizzie's parents are here today. They are talking to Ian. I have always found Lizzie's parents really positive towards me. Both of them were civil engineers and made a real success of it. Her dad, Jorge, had retired early and he and Carmen saw a lot of Ian and Susie and Lizzie's sister's children.

Carol isn't here today, she and her kids have gone on a holiday but her ex, Michael, is. I'm guessing that he has to put in an appearance, with his new girlfriend. She (Sara, did she say?) is a lot younger than Michael and is clearly wondering why they are here, although she did bring a lovely wreath and seems nice enough. Michael, though, is breaking the 'half your age plus seven' rule by some distance.

Lizzie is being pleasant to Michael but struggling to be so with Sara. Fair enough, and I will have to follow suit. The kids though are pleased to see Uncle Michael even so and can't be expected to subscribe to adult disapproval protocols. In Sara, also, they have found someone closer to their age and that is always fun at events like this. They go off and are substituted at the table by Laura and Zoe.

I think Laura is bearing up well. Like Lizzie, Zoe has been amazingly supportive, although she always is. Laura's speech at the funeral was much better than mine, not that it is a competition. She talked about the moments in Mum's life that mattered, about the lack of judgement Mum had brought to her sexuality. She had spoken to all of Mum's friends before the funeral and talked about their thoughts of Mum. She was funny too, but in a lovely way.

I am not great at well timed, or subtle, humour. I can do serious, or jokey, but not at the same time. I need to know whether the audience is taking me seriously or wants to be amused. If I get a choice I usually go for the amusing, I find it easier than sincere, although the line between amusing and rude is not always that clear to me. My groom's speech at Lizzie and my wedding was so rude about her that Jorge got quite cross. He doesn't usually get cross, so I knew I had gone too far.

The same was true at work. I have a tendency to express my view strongly and not worry about who I might upset along the way. I know not to do that with clients but with colleagues I feel we should all be able to speak our minds. My colleagues would hopefully acknowledge that I am more often right than wrong. It did not follow that saying it was the best way to achieve something. It took me many (too many) years to realise that this could be a problem and an impediment to my career, and even more to work out that with clients I was role playing a lawyer so didn't mind so much what they thought of me, but with my colleagues, I was being judged.

Mum always used to say exactly what she thought too. I guess I got it from her.

***

"It's really kind of you to agree to take Dad in," Laura says to Lizzie.

"It's no problem, we always said we would if your mum got too difficult to look after. Ian and Susie will love having him, and we've got the room."

"Even so, we really do appreciate it. I was talking to your parents just now. It's really kind of them to come. They seem really well. How are they?"

"They are fine, getting on a bit, but still able to cope with the house in Richmond. They are bit cross with Carol. With the fact that she still took the kids away on holiday, but I guess she just didn't want to see Michael."

"And his new woman?'

"Yes."

"It's given Zoe all sorts of ideas about finding someone like that for herself," laughs Laura.

"Shut up Laura, you'll always be the one for me."

All three of them laugh. Dad looks over. I smile at him and get a sort of wince back. I get up to go over and chat to him.

***

It is raining now, a day too late, but consistent with most of my memories of this place. Dad and I have come to scatter Mum's ashes on the Gower. Laura had wanted to come but had a recital to deliver in London so had said her goodbyes that morning. We set off early, stopped at the crematorium to collect the ashes, paused for breakfast at a service station, crossed the bridge at noon and are now stood on the headland above Caswell Bay. The grey sea is breaking on the rocks below, while moody clouds hang disapprovingly over them. And the rain is falling in sheets. This is more like it: the planet is recognising the loss of one of its own.

"This was where Mum was at her happiest," I say.

"Yes, despite the weather. Your Mum and I went to the Caribbean once."

"I remember."

"And she said it just like a less beautiful Gower, except the sea was blue."

"And warm."

"And warm."

131

I thought the service was lovely," he says.

"Yes, although I am not sure about having a humanist one. That lets God off the hook."

"What do you mean?" asks Dad.

"Well, it's his fault, he set the whole thing up."

"I want a proper funeral in a church."

"Not yet though."

"Not yet no," he says, "I have lots of things to do still, and I am really looking forward to coming to live with you, Lizzie and the kids."

"We are looking forward to having you?"

"Are you sure it's OK?"

"Of course, it'll be great, and what Mum would have wanted."

"You don't think Mum would have wanted me to suffer a bit after she had gone, at least for a while?"

"You looked after her for five years after her stroke. I don't know whether she ever said anything to you, but she said to me, and Laura, how amazing you had been."

"No, she never said, that is nice to hear though."

"It's like she would never tell me whether she was proud of me, but she would tell Laura she was."

"And she would tell me how proud she was of both of you."

"Didn't want us getting uppity."

"No, and fair enough, she never was. Your Mum was one of the humblest people I have ever met. I loved her for it, although sometimes I think it was partly learnt from the hard time she had with her parents and as a working woman. I am going to miss her. Looking after her was my main mission in life."

"So now we can look after you."

"Shall I get the ashes from the car?"

"Yes, and the flowers."

"Don't fall off the edge while I am gone."

"Do you think I am going to jump?"

"No, but its windy and wet so be careful."

"Sure, see you in a minute."

We throw the white lilies and black ash into the wind and rain. Like two ancient Druids invoking the gods of sand and sea. No gods come but a proper burial has been made.

The Iraq war continues to have terrible consequences for the people of that region, the London Olympics are a major, although expensive, success. Barack is re-elected and Ian goes to University. Followed by Susie a couple of years later.

15 October 2014

I put her last suitcase in the boot of the car.

"Bye honey," says Lizzie.

"Bye honey," I say (the old ones are the best etc.).

"I meant Susie," says Lizzie.

"I think he knew that Mum," says Susie.

They hug and Susie and I get in the car.

I am taking Susie to University. It's been one of my jobs with Ian and now there are two of them to ferry, to different places of course. It is one of my pleasures. Three hours with one of the kids and doing something useful, and for them.

While Ian and I would occupy the majority of the time with sports discussion, with Susie it's politics. Not just because that's what she's studying. It's what really interests her. I think she is going to be prime minister one day. She would laugh at that because she thinks the current system doesn't work. She is talking about launching a party herself – the Future Party – which would look to get things done which represent the needs of the young, those for whom the future is being built - votes

133

for sixteen-year-olds, addressing house prices, technology training – those sorts of things. It sounds great but, apparently, I am too old to join. I could be a "friend" though!

Susie's favourite topic, and therefore mine (?), is gender politics. I sometimes think I won't qualify for her party on the grounds of my gender as well as my age.

By the time we get to the Luton junction (birthplace, but I have never gone back) we are debating the role of men these days.

"Maybe that's not the question. What is anyone's role these days?" I suggest.

"OK, but let's start with men. You grew up in a traditional two parent family, both your parents worked but the way you talk, Grandad clearly had the "career" while Grandma had a job."

"I guess, and at home the tasks split along traditional gender lines – Mum cooked, Dad drove, Mum washed and ironed, Dad gardened and grew vegetables. At school, there were boys, who played sports, and girls who did their hair and got pursued by the boys."

"I assume girls did sports too, just not your sports."

"Fair enough. Boys fought, girls didn't. Boys looked at porn, girls didn't."

"Again I suggest that is your perception, not the reality."

"You are probably right, but I definitely grew up with a very traditional view."

"You did, didn't you!" laughs Susie.

"But you got better, is that Mum's influence?"

"Maybe. It's also probably two other things: I went to university and came across all those active feminist groups; and later my big sister, my favourite woman in the world at the time, told me she was gay. Both, in their ways, explained to me that the traditional allocation of roles and assumptions about

134

how the sexes would behave was sexist and derived from generations of prejudice."

"And bad behaviour by men and straight people."

"I am not sure it is that simple, but I did and do readily accept the right of women to equal treatment and the right of gay people to equality with straights."

"That's very big of you!" she snorts.

"But what do you mean by equal and equality?"

"Ah, now I am going to fall down. I do think my original views were pretty unsophisticated. Now, later in life, they aren't much more sophisticated, but I do think it is complex, beyond the slogans."

"What do you mean?"

"So: it is not so clear to me what equality really means and how, in practice, to ensure everyone gets an equal life chance, regardless of their background/gender/sexual preference/race/religion."

"For example?"

"Well, take the gender issue. It seems to me that Lizzie, Laura, you and maybe when she was alive, my Mum, although less so, have much of the ability to be happy and successful that I, Ian and Dad do. Arguably, all of you, again, maybe not my Mum, seem to me to be happier than me. So, the bias and prejudice has not paid off for me."

"But it has though. In so many invisible ways. And the women in your life are exceptional."

"Of course, in many ways!"

I had read an essay of Susie's over the Summer holidays that she had written as part of her politics A level.

Can there be a ceasefire with men or do women need to win the war?

It sounded a bit aggressive. It was.

In the introduction, she had written:

The life chances of a white clever middle class straight man are greater than those who are not one, or more, of those things.

There has been some progress, but society isn't going to fix things quickly so there has to be a mechanism to overcome that lack of equality, something beyond the much-maligned political correctness.

You have to watch your language and definitely go out of your way to be sensitive to others. But that means more than just knowing when not to express "ist" thoughts: it ultimately means not thinking them, or more realistically, recognising them in yourself and acting to change. It also means calling out against the behaviours and language of others.

There is so much more to it than that. If organisations and societies are not going to achieve representative leadership teams and workforces and communities then there has to be action to make it happen.

Those views, although theoretically simple and straightforward, just take us to the real debates around some of the subtler complexities. What if the rights of one group could only be promoted by the suppression of the rights of another?

Can you have positive promotion of women at work, without slowing down the career progression of men?

Clearly not, it is a zero-sum game but that one is relatively simple; everyone's career prospects are always suppressed by someone else; this is just less arbitrary.

What about the Palestinian question, though, where all left-wing sympathies but not all the arguments are with the Palestinians?

Or the tolerance of religious or cultural practices, which are regarded as illiberal? If the bible tells a believer to be a homophobe, aren't you suppressing them if they are not allowed to express it or even, I should argue, think it?

It is really a question of social evolution. You have to

have a sense of destination and then evaluate everything as whether it takes steps towards or away from that destination

The ultimate destination should really be one of love and respect and happiness for all. It is not equality of opportunity; it is equality of outcome. Everyone is entitled to love, and respect and happiness. Of course, it is underpinned by some more basic goals, like freedom from war, starvation, disease, none of which are consistent with human happiness. It is also dependent, in theory at least, on someone knowing which actions will move us in the right direction.

But if those actions result in protests or violence by another group that perceive a wrong, then the conditions to avoid that need to be created before the action is taken.

That requires the oppressors to lay down their arms first.

As I say, a bit scary. And too complicated to understand after the introduction. I did ask her whether she really believed it, to that extent.

She thought about the question and said, gently.

"It's all very complex in practice, but not in theory no. And it's all got to happen, not just be debated on my way to university, or in my politics classes."

"OK, I hope you can get it done."

"We are all going to get it done."

I hope she's right.

25 December 2014

"King Kong, It's King Kong!" shouts Susie.

I point at her "You're right, three points for our team!" and I high five her.

We are playing charades, a Piper Christmas day tradition: pillowcases in bed, breakfast, presents, lunch, charades, Monopoly, family arguments, TV, Lizzie's parents for Boxing Day.

Charades is harder now, given the age range playing. Dad has started introducing musicals from the 1950s, while Ian and Susie watch TV programmes that the rest of us have never heard of. So we have rewritten the rules, two teams, clues picked for the other team, no really obscure stuff.

I am on a team with Susie, and Zoe. Lizzie has got Dad, Ian and Laura. Lizzie's team have given us King Kong, Hard Times, Terminator, Watership Down and The Clangers. Zoe's Clanger whistling had been brilliantly identifiable. Lizzie had to explain to Susie that Watership Down was about rabbits, so that she could do the "whole thing".

Lizzie had bought everyone onesies and I was delighted with my Baloo (the Jungle Book bear), although I am not sure Laura liked her Incredible Hulk so much. Lizzie had chosen Wonder Woman for herself. Given that she had bought all the kids' presents, as well those for Dad, Laura and Zoe it seemed appropriate, although I had wrapped them all. I got Lizzie a handbag for Christmas and a new toaster. While the toaster was really cool (how cool can a toaster be, actually?), I had not really planned well. Letting Lizzie open it first did not help the mood and by the time the handbag arrived I was in the "men!" house.

I tried to cook lunch by way of redemption, although Lizzie had been the one to get up at 5 am to put the oven on, and I also had to hand over the reins towards the end. I had been fast asleep at 5 am, having stayed up late last night, watching Aliens, again. Sigourney Weaver is on my laminated card – the people you can sleep with without your spouse kicking off – along with Chrissie Hynde, Julia Roberts, Charlotte Church (a bit young for me though) and Helen Mirren. Lizzie has Clive Owen, Russell Brand and George Clooney, along with two ex-boyfriends, which bothers me slightly. Apparently, according to Laura, if you are gay you have a slightly different card, one that lists the people of the opposite sex who were so sexy that you would have straight sex with them.

Maybe straight people should have the other sort of card as well; which men would be on mine? Maybe Russell Brand?

We used to try and go away for Christmas, to somewhere warmer, where someone else cooked lunch for you, but the kids never enjoyed it as much as Christmas at home and now they were at an age where they wanted to get back to hanging out with their mates as soon after the festivities as possible. And Dad doesn't really travel well, so a London staycation it is. Most of our friends do the same but many of them then go skiing over New Year. We have only been skiing once, when the kids were young. Lizzie quite enjoyed it, and is quite a good skier, but I find the whole falling, or being run, over dispiriting, wet and cold. Even the chairlift confounded me when it didn't stop for me to get off at the top. What if elevators did that?

I remember one that did. It was at my University. The building must have been twenty floors and to travel up and down you literally had to get into, and out of, the open human boxes while they kept moving. The system had some sort of special name – a Paternoster lift - and I often wondered what would happen if I stayed in until the top. Would I be crushed as the boxes flattened out, or tipped upside down before descending? I never tried it, but I was mildly surprised that I never heard of anyone else doing so. Maybe you got flattened at the top and no-one ever found you, until they did periodic maintenance and found several crushed students that we all though had dropped out?

It is Ian's turn. He picks up one and starts. A film. One word. He points at me, and then at the TV – "Aliens" says

Lizzie, knowing what I had watched last night. I had written that one, thinking it was tough. Ian is smart, as is Susie, although they both carry it in a confident and pleasant way. That is their mother's doing, mainly, although I like to believe that I have contributed to some of the things that the kids think.

They both bought me a book for Christmas – Suggs' autobiography from Ian and an Amis (Kingsley not Martin) from Susie. Lizzie gave me cufflinks - the new socks - although they were lovely. The kids had mainly had electronic and digital stuff, most of it made by Apple and involving the letter "i".

I try to keep the balance right with technology. On the one hand, I don't want to be seen as a Luddite but, on the other, unlike many others, mostly men in my experience, I don't feel the need to be able to talk about the half-life of knowledge travelling towards the singularity either. Apart from anything else, doesn't that mean that, at some point in the future, we will all know only one thing forever?

I really, really have no idea what I just said means. I resisted the lure of "i-things" for as long as I could and stuck to my Blackberry – another fruit though – and I still read books and newspapers in handleable form. I do own an iPad but basically use it as a portable television – now there's an idea! Despite this techresister stance, I did quickly try to adopt txt spk, so as to appear cool to the kids. Lots of LOL, smiley faces and the occasional one I make up just to intrigue or confound them. My favourite is WDYMT – What Does Your Mother Think?

Their mother thinks it's time that we should all clear the lunch dishes away, so the game of charades comes to an end.

I start to clear away the dishes. Lizzie and Laura are in the kitchen laughing. The kids are with Zoe and Dad.

140

"Did you fight in the war, Grandad?"

Susie is studying the politics of the Cold War this semester.

"No, I was too young to fight in the war, but I did join the army after the war to do National Service."

"What's National Service?"

"Well, a long time ago, even when there wasn't a war on you had to serve in the army for two years after your seventeenth birthday."

"So, I would be there now?"

"No, it was men only."

"Why?"

"That's how things were then, people thought women shouldn't fight."

"Maybe more women in the army would have led to fewer wars," enquired Susie with a grin.

"Maybe."

I knew Dad had done National Service, in Singapore and Malaysia. He has told the kids before about the marching and the heat and the pointless training runs. How he had ridden an elephant and fired his rifle at lots of targets. I had heard different versions of this story before.

A couple of Christmases ago, I found Dad, in his bedroom, crying. I assumed it was over Mum.

"Are you OK dad?"

"I just had a letter from Australia. A friend of mine died."

He showed me a black and white photograph, of four young men, in army uniform, stood beside a sign saying, "Kuala Lumpur 200 miles". I recognise Dad, he looks incredibly young, younger than the kids.

"That's Mike," he says, pointing at the man to the left of him. "His wife sent me a letter last week telling me that he has died. I haven't seen him for nearly sixty years, but we wrote

141

to each other every year. We served together in the Army in Singapore."

While Dad had been too young to fight in the War, he had done his basic army training and then been sent to Singapore to do his National Service in 1948. That I knew: what I didn't know was what they had been out there to do.

Now he was telling Susie and Ian, and me. I have never heard this bit, or asked, before.

Dad had worked in the paymaster's office, which meant, amongst other things, that he paid out bonuses to his colleagues for "extra duty". The "extra duties" were the execution of Japanese War criminals or the killing of Malay Chinese insurgents. World War Two had been brutal in South East Asia but that brutality had not stopped in 1945. He had to go to Changi Jail one time and witness three Japanese officers being hanged. He never fired his rifle in anger, but he saw dozens of bodies while he was out there.

The first Christmas they were out there, he explained, he had been given a two-day furlough, along with most of his squad. The plan was to go for some R&R in a camp over the border in Malaya. There were ten of them, including him and Mike, and they travelled in two jeeps. It took most of the day to get there, along the dusty roads, through the heat and local traffic. There were few vehicles - mainly local people and their animals. They arrived at the camp just before dusk, were cleared by the guards, and grabbed some sleep in the cabins. There were a couple of other groups there also.

Breakfast was served in a couple of tents behind the cabins. There was also a ready supply of cigarettes, local beers, cards, sports equipment and swimming gear – the camp had a 50-foot swimming pool, complete with diving board.

Dad had never learnt to swim so stayed in the tents playing cards with Mike, and a couple of guys from the Royal Engineers. Mike heard it first –the sound of shooting – they

142

assumed it was out at the firing range. But it didn't sound that far away. They left the tent and ran to the cabins to get their rifles. Two of the camp guards ran past them. "Get in the cabins and stay there!" one of them shouted.

They should have done so, but by the time they had their rifles and emerged, the shooting had stopped anyway. Making their way cautiously down to the pool, they saw the results of the insurgent attack. Three of their squad were lying dead in the pool, and there were maybe half a dozen others injured. They, Dad included, jumped into the pool to retrieve the men. There were three Malay Chinese bodies near the woods behind the pool. That was presumably where they had come from. Apparently there had been seven or eight of them. They had emerged from the trees, firing on the soldiers in the pool. Once the guards had arrived, they had retreated, losing three on the way.

Dad and Mike travelled back to Singapore in the military ambulance with a couple of the injured. Dad knew he would be paying out more bonuses when they sent a large force after the perpetrators.

15 August 2015

"What do you want dad?" asks Ian.

"A pint of lager, I don't mind which. Something not too strong."

"Grandad?"

"Just a coke, thanks."

It is still two hours until kick off, and I don't want to drink too much before the game. Not that that seems to be stopping the rest of the pub. Most of them look like they have been here since noon, or earlier, and are well on their way.

Fair enough, though, we have something to celebrate. Watford are back in the premiership and this is the first home game of the season. Not a very glamorous tie – West Bromwich Albion (with all due respect to the people of that fine town, or city, or whatever it is, is it a bit of Birmingham?) – but we haven't been in this division for a few years, so we are going to enjoy it.

Ian and I used to go to see Watford together when he was younger. We had season tickets for maybe ten years. It always seemed slightly cruel to him that he had to grow up as a fan of a team, which was unlikely to win much, unless its Italian owners sold it to a billionaire. But that's football for you, or maybe all sports. You establish loyalty early on to one of the team you or friends played for, or the one you grew up watching and supporting and/or your country.

So Ian supports Finchley rugby club, although he hasn't played for them for a couple of years, Watford and England (yes, England!) in football, rugby and most other sports. Supporting England internationally is a bit like supporting Watford, although their women got to the semi-final of the world cup a couple of months ago. Even Lizzie and Susie had got excited about football then. To be clear, I say "even" not because women don't get men's football but in relation to Lizzie and Susie themselves. Lizzie will come along if there is lunch and entertainment alongside the football, but the terraces at Vicarage Road offer neither. I did take Susie with Ian a couple of times, but she used to watch the scoreboard to see what was going on. They both used to come along and watch Ian when he played rugby though.

My Dad isn't really into football, although we have been to a couple of games since he moved to London and he has avidly followed Watford's season this year. Ian bought him a Watford calendar for Christmas, which he has loyally used as his primary organiser.

My support is slightly more complicated than Ian's. I have never really played sport properly. I was born in Luton, in

England. Yet I support Watford and Wales. I never thought about supporting England, I am Welsh – I grew up there and my parents are Welsh - although I am not sufficiently Welsh, or anti-England, to wish them ill unless they are playing Wales at something. In football, that usually meant watching England fail to achieve much every couple of years.

For once though, Wales are playing great, or effective, football and are currently top of the table for the Euro 2016 qualifiers. No doubt we will fall back after an embarrassing 1-0 loss to Andorra. It has been nearly 60 years since we qualified for a tournament.

Supporting Watford is even more complicated. I used to support Luton Town, on the basis there were no decent Welsh teams, for many years. Not in a very active way but, nevertheless, until I was in my early forties, if you asked me who I supported I would have said Luton and I could credibly do the required five minutes on their team and their prospects, like any other self-respecting man. Again, I am not being sexist, it's just that football seems to me one of the most male things, or maybe a substitute for male things?

In the 1990s Luton Town football club was taken over by a couple of local politicians and businessmen who many regarded as racist. I had no idea about that at the time nor of the truth of that claim. In 2005 we moved out to Hertfordshire and Watford was our closest club. So, Ian and I went along. Again, through my ignorance, I knew nothing of the enmity between Watford and Luton, my former club.

I have, however, rewritten the history of my disloyalty in a way that sometimes even I believe my story. As I tell it, as a good left winger (although not in a football sense –see what I did there!), with my political consciousness, how could I continue to support them when they were run by racists? Determined to show how strongly I felt, I claim that I rejected them and decided to support their arch enemy. It was, I say, a purely theoretical support, not one that made a real impact on Luton's or Watford's finances, nor registered with the owners of the club, until we moved nearby.

So when Ian was old enough, we could go and see "my" team and I had a convincing backstory for anyone who remembered my support of the Hatters. And now we are hooked. Luton recently fell out of the Football League and maybe that just goes to show what happens when you get involved with racists!

"So what do you reckon the score will be?" Dad asks.

"Two nil to us," says Ian, handing over our drinks.

"With lots of 'Premier League, you're having a laugh', chanting by the West Brom fans," I add.

Chanting and singing at football matches has always been a bit of oddity for me. It has none of the quality of the singing at rugby games, particularly Welsh ones and, I guess, I did not grow up listening to it. Ian has and he joins in with gusto. I enjoy it but, also unlike rugby, every team seems to have the same chants and songs.

Whether it is something to 'when the saints come marching in', or the ironic "You're not singing any more" or the one that doesn't even scan but claims your team are "the best the world has ever seen". I guess its loyalty to your tribe, as its handpicked and well-paid gladiators fight it out in the arena for you.

Of course those football supporter tribes themselves used to be more actively involved in the fighting. I am not trying to defend it, but it makes some sense. If your tribe is being attacked then you have to defend yourself and the pride from being a tribal member is tangible for many.

Thirty years or more ago, these boys' tribes or gangs existed wherever you looked. It was based on your team, or your music or the way you dressed or, maybe more understandably but worryingly, your class, or your race, or

146

politics. It wasn't always only boys, but we do seem to have some need to join, to belong, at least until we have our own family to be part of. Our parents aren't our family, they are the tribal elders you have to overthrow, or run away from. In many cases even after our own family arrives, we men seem to continue to need a tribal outlet.

The crowd in the pub spans all ages and races. That is a very definite improvement from twenty years ago, but there are still very few women. Lots of fathers and sons, lots of twenty something mates, lots of middle-aged men with XXL team shirts.

I sometimes go to see football matches on my own – being a Watford fan there isn't huge demand for my other season ticket. I will watch the fans in the pub before the game and speculate about their lives. There are lots of tattoos – tribal markings. Twenty years ago, men with tattoos meant danger and violence, now it is cool, as is sticking stuff in your face, or those weird earrings that make holes so big that you can hang the owner up on the coat rack by them.

I have nothing against any of this. It is fascinating and cool. If I see someone who looks safe, I sometimes offer them my spare ticket and have a fellow fan for the day. A couple of times I was asked if I had two, which didn't really work. Although I did, once, when asked by a young woman, give her both, pretending my own seat was in a different part of the ground and hanging out in the pub until the usual home time.

Today though we are using both tickets and I have also got one for my Dad. I will let Ian and him sit together and use the spare one myself, surrounded by a sea of men, tattoos, and tributes to the eyesight of the referee.

The world went weird, or maybe just even weirder. Jeremy Corbyn inherited the Labour Party. We voted, just, for Brexit. Wales not only qualified for, but almost won, a football tournament. And Donald Trump became president of the United States.

11 June 2017

It is the same every time I see him these days. We have settled into a routine.

"I'm your son, Dad."

"My son?"

"Yes."

"I have a son?"

"Yes, and a daughter and two grandchildren."

I show him their pictures on my phone.

"And a wife?"

"Yes, although she died."

"My wife's dead? Oh no. When did she die?"

Tears well up in his eyes.

It always starts like this. Sometimes just once, and he holds on to the knowledge that I am his son, or at least a family member, for the whole visit. Sometimes it repeats itself throughout. Today he is more confused than usual, so we are repeating the routine every fifteen minutes or so. If he doesn't ask about Mum I don't volunteer the information, but he usually does. I used to be vague, or, I would argue, not upset him by telling him she had died. But I feel better (does he?) if I don't lie to him.

We are sat in the garden of his home. He is in his wheelchair. When we first came to the home, he didn't need one and we did pay for a physiotherapist to come and see him once a week to do his exercises with him. Over time though, he got less mobile and, eventually, it just became easier to let him wheel himself around.

"How are you, Dad?"

"OK."

"When am I coming back to your house?"

"You were there, last weekend, for Sunday lunch."

"Was I?"

"We watched the tennis together."

"I used to play tennis."

"I know. You were quite good. You taught me to play."

"Do you still play?"

"Not really."

"That's a pity, I used to enjoy playing tennis. And I was quite good."

"I know."

"Is your house near here?" he asks.

"About a mile away."

"Do you have a garden?

"Yes."

"Is it like this one?"

"Yes, although a bit smaller."

"Yes, this is a nice size garden. Although it needs weeding a bit."

"Maybe you could help with that."

"We both could, why don't you get your tools, and we'll do it."

"Ok, let me do that later."

Dad used to love to garden. It was his favourite place to be. He didn't have a very big garden – nothing like the garden in this home, nor the size of ours now. But he managed to cram a lot in and always find work that needed doing, planting, weeding, and harvesting the fruit and veg, pelleting the slugs, mowing the lawn. It is one of the reasons we chose this home for him. The garden is lovely and, despite Dad's comment re weeding, it is kept really nice. Most of the residents seem to be out in it today but it is still not crowded. Dad and I are sat in the shade – the sun is too hot for him. Me sat on a bench. Him in his chair. He looks happy enough.

149

It's hard to tell. He seems to spend most of his time either eating – three proper meals a day - or sleeping, in bed, in his chair. He doesn't really join in the activities and was never one for reading a lot or watching TV – we got one for his room, but it is rarely on. It's no good asking him what he's been doing, or what time he got up, or whether he has had lunch yet, he won't know. But, unlike what we hear from some of our friends about their parents, he never seems distressed or angry. He seems dressed OK and they have shaved him recently. No doubt the pills he takes are in part responsible for his seeming calm and early on we did worry that the home are medicating him into submission rather than tranquillity.

I also tried harder early on to really connect with him, to find out how he was feeling, where he thought he was, what he wanted. Tough to push him that hard and tough to hear the stuff about wanting to just die now. I guess that's why we don't talk about it anymore.

The lunch bell sounds.

"Are you hungry Dad?"

"Yes."

We go back in from the garden, and I push him to his seat at his usual lunch table.

"Hello, Mister Sandpiper," says Theresa.

Dad and Theresa always sit at the same table.

"How are you today?" she asks.

"Fine. You?"

"Fine, I am getting out today."

"Really, that's great."

"Can you take my dad with you?"

"Of course," she says.

Another well-rehearsed routine.

I kiss my Dad on the forehead.

"Have a nice lunch Dad, I love you."

"I love you too."

It's not always easy. It's never easy.

We still have my dad's butterfly and stamp collections. They are stored with his other stuff in boxes in our attic. They were in his room but, once he had moved into the home, we cleared them into the roof. He managed three years with us after Mum died but it was increasingly difficult (for him, or us?) so we fell in with the middle class, middle-aged way of things and found him a care home. It's a nice home, as care homes go, although that is from my perspective, not his. To the extent he has a perspective anymore, "nice" is probably not the word.

It is OK, the staff do the best they can.

It's not really, but I have to think it's OK, don't I? To be fair to the staff I do think they do well, they are paid very little to look after other people's parents. But he's my dad, my family. Laura doesn't like it at all, but she travels around too much to have him. At least she comes to see him almost every week. I am less regular. Lizzie says she would still have him if I would look after him and warns me that Ian and Susie will see how I treat him and treat me the same later. How do I reconcile all that?

He has a room full of photos of us all. We have written him a note outlining who he is and who we are. The difference between his Alzheimer's and those people who have the five minute or one hour memory is, I am sure, medically significant. Practically though I am not sure what difference it makes.

Sometimes I take him to the pub. He always has a glass of wine and an ice cream.

Getting him there is often a struggle. He is more often than not in bed and had been last weekend. He had also soiled himself and so I had to shower him before we went.

This is the man who used to carry me on his shoulders, tickle me until I cried and wrestle me with one hand behind his back. Now he has both hands behind his back, needs a

151

wheelchair and has forgotten everything he knew.

I love him but I don't want to see this too often and I don't want to end up like him. I wish he hadn't ended up like this either. I think, or hope, that most of the time he doesn't think like that himself but sometimes, just sometimes, I know he does.

Last weekend, as I put him back to bed, full of Shiraz and vanilla, he grabbed me by the wrist.

"Thanks for coming to see me. Don't come back again. I want to die now and you coming to see me just interrupts me."

15 April 2018

So I lost my Dad a while before he actually died. Long before the day the home called to say he had passed away in his sleep, Laura and I had agreed that he was no longer there. His memory loss became a personality loss. He didn't seem to be uncomfortable or distressed, instead we were, and my visits became less and less frequent.

We had a proper religious funeral, like he wanted. Other than the immediate family, the only other attendees were some staff and other residents from the home. Laura played Dad's favourite Bach concerto and Ian and Susie said some really nice things about him, and about their mum and dad.

This time Laura drove to the Gower.

Brexit ploughed on, England lost two football World Cups and won one in cricket. Boris Johnson became prime minister, and won an election. (Shouldn't that have to happen the other way around?) Piers Morgan claimed to be a penguin.

11 December 2019

Woke has become a bit of an issue and battleground. As my contribution, I tried to write a counter piece to Piers and his penguin rant.

One hundred types of penguin

Piers Morgan's full name is Piers Stefan Phone Hacker (I made that bit up) Pughe-Morgan and he used to be an O'Meara. So, he has quality Celtic roots, which should have stood him in good stead to understand that not everyone is a posh cis boy from Surrey. Where did it all go wrong?

We don't have the time.

Anyway, Piers was apparently triggered into claiming to be a "two spirit pan gender" penguin by a story about a non-binary penguin chick at London Zoo and one of his interviewees claiming that there are not just two or three genders but 100.

Gender fluidity is the latest in a long and respectable line of development of sophistication and nuance in how we think about others. Given there are 7 billion of us it is surprising to me that there are only 100 gender types. Piers, and some others, need to accept and learn that while they crudely stereotype diversity as an obsession of woke snowflakes, it is really about respecting difference and wanting the best for all.

In reality, what bothers me is that their real viewpoint

153

is that even if individuals other than the traditional straight, Christian, cis boy or girl do exist, they should not. That is what it is really about.

How can we debate the merits of their argument?

Well, like Piers, I have chosen to pursue the argument through the use of allegory. Are there, and should there be, 100 types of penguin?

So how many penguins are there from which we have to find our 100? There are 40 million penguins in the world, of which about a third live in Antarctica.

They used to populate the whole Earth but, over time, they have slid downwards on the ice so that now all but a couple of thousand Galapagos penguins live south of the equator. There are maybe 20 species and subspecies of each.

Let us start with what is a penguin. Or, to be more accurate, a cis penguin, so a penguin born that way, who self identifies as one.

To keep it very simple, like those who think there are just men and women, living creatures are really only animals, birds or fish. Birds fly, fish swim and animals walk or run? So a penguin isn't a bird, because it does not fly? It has flippers and does swim, so maybe it is a fish? Or it has feet, so it is an animal? Can it be all three? Does it matter? I think you would need to ask them.

I do not think they have been asked. Nor do I even know how we would, but I think we should assume that they do not care, so nor should we. Maybe they think of themselves as penguin animals when on land and penguin fish when in water? They even have different names for a group of them when on land - a waddle, rude I think but accurate - and, when at sea, a raft.

Maybe some species of penguin think of themselves as animals and regard other, lesser, penguin species as fish?

I bet the Emperor and King penguin think they are

154

animals and look down on the fairy and small blue fish penguins. And no one thinks to ask the Empress and Queen penguins what they think.

What do the Macaroni or Gentoo penguins think they are, animals, fish, the unicorns of the penguin world?

How do gender and species politics play out in the penguin world?

In our human world, women are, of course, left behind because they have to carry our children around for such a long period of time that the men have got ahead by the time the women give birth. Not the case for penguins. Mum penguin lays an egg and that's it, they are back to the sea for two months while the dad carries the egg around on his feet. No football for him. And no food until the egg hatches, so actually fat boy penguins are the most sought after as they can last long enough for the egg to hatch.

What about the species, is there "ichthyosognoy" in the penguin world? Look it up. I have combined fear of fish and the sogony part of misogony. Is there species'd behaviour?

Penguins seem more interested in their own species than picking on others. There are very rare Isabelline penguins, which are brown rather than black. Again penguins seem to leave them alone, rather than obsessing with the difference. All in all, they seem much more evolved than us humans.

Maybe Piers would have be much more tolerant if he was a cis Celtic penguin?

Pingu Morgan anyone?

On 31 December 2019, woke and Trump and Johnson and lots of other stuff took a back seat. China informed the World Health Organisation of a novel coronavirus outbreak in the city of Wuhan.

23 March 2020

We are being locked down. This is extraordinary, and a little bit scary and even the football has been suspended.

Easter Sunday 2020

"There are rhinos everywhere!" I cry. "How are we going to get out of this?"

Lizzie, Ian and I are trapped in some sort of sports hall. To get away we need to get to the road behind the fence. But there are three rhinos patrolling the area between the hall and the fence. I did look out of the back door but there is another rhino, maybe the biggest of all, sat on the grass watching us.

I have no idea how we got here, or where Susie is. All I know is the barricade we made with our cars won't be strong enough to withstand things when they attack.

I wake. Another dream, this time about rhinos.

It is day 103 of 2020, and day 25 of Lockdown.

I collected Susie and Ian from their flats about a month ago. Most of their friends have gone home to their parents too. And Ling is with us as she can't go back to China. Susie has a new boyfriend, Jake. We haven't met him yet. If he lasts long enough I am sure we will, but not at the moment as he is self-isolating with his parents in South London. Seems a bit unfair on Susie to have no one with her but they all spend their time in constant contact anyway.

It's Facebook, or Snapchat (not so much anymore apparently), WhatsApp. Instagram, Tik Tok, Houseparty, Zoom and Your Own Little World (I made that one up). Lizzie and I have adopted some of these before so as to vaguely keep in touch with the kids and to appear hip with our friends. Lizzie much more than me. I am only really on LinkedIn, which I think is from the 20th Century and mainly consists of people

156

making or liking corporate postings. They were all about diversity, then climate change, and now they are about thanking the NHS and how to deliver virtual workshops.

Having woken, I will get up, even though its Easter Sunday. A routine has been established already. As the only one still with work to do, I get up at seven every morning and am in bed by ten. Ian, Ling, Susie and Lizzie are around for the second half of my day. To be fair, maybe slightly longer, they are all up by noonish and we sit down for a meal. By then I will have got my unhealthy stuff - coffee, cigarettes, toast and cheese, wine gums sometimes - out of the way. And we all have healthy largely vegetarian but, to be fair, delicious meals.

Today is no different. No sign of anyone else, I have had two coffees, three cigarettes and a bowl of Coco Pops by ten. With no video calls today, I guess I will wait until the others are up before we have a vegan Easter Egg hunt.

These are weird, and scary times. We think all of us have had the virus, although as there is no testing, how do we know? Lizzie went down with it first and spent a week in bed, followed by me. The youngsters all lost their sense of taste and smell for what seemed like ten minutes. I have stopped drinking for the month now, without any ill effects, but seem incapable of stopping smoking. How I reconcile that to a virus that attacks your lungs is not entirely clear to me. Although, in a weird way, I have come into my own.

Now everybody is thinking about dying every day, not just me. And, sadly, some of them are dying. We lost nearly 1,000 people yesterday in the UK, and over 100,000 are reported to have died globally. I am sure that is a massive underreport, although how much no one knows.

If our infection curve comes down soon then maybe we can see our way to easing the lockdown by the end of April? And we will have to cancel Brexit now, or at least postpone it?

17 May 2020

Lockdown is supposed to be a time during which we all take on new hobbies and self-development. I try writing a short story.

A Corona Tale

We are at the Emirates Stadium, sitting in the posh seats, but our heart is with the away fans down below.

"Come on Watford," we scream, in our heads, as we will get thrown out if we show our true colours.

They need this. Deeney steps up, strikes it to the left and…

<u>*Two weeks earlier.*</u>

Ian comes into the kitchen.

"Have you seen the PL announcement? They have cancelled the rest of the season."

I haven't seen the Premier League announcement. I Google it.

So, Liverpool have been declared champions. Fair enough.

"Watford have been relegated!"

"What do you mean we have been relegated? We were 17th when the season stopped."

"I know but they have used a head to head formula to calculate the end of season positions, we are 18th on goal difference. Aston Villa stayed up instead of us."

"Fuck… that's not fair."

"I know."

It's one thing the country being locked down and the economy destroyed. It's another Watford being relegated. My day, day 39 of lockdown, is spoiled.

158

Six months earlier.

"I don't feel very well. I am going home," Shi says to her assistant.

Shi Zhengi is the head of the Wuhan Research Laboratory Complex.

She is in the Chiropteran Lab. Chiroptera is the scientific name for bats.

"Ok boss," says Chang. "I hope you feel better soon. Should we carry on with the centrifuges?"

"Yes, but be careful. I'm sure it's just a bug. I will be back in tomorrow."

She swipes out of the lab and the building and gets into her car, a blue Volkswagen Santana. It will take an hour to get home. Shi lives with her husband, Yi, on the fifth floor or a new apartment block, Crane Tower, in Zhangjia Bay Residential District, overlooking the Yangtze. It is a lovely apartment.

10,000 miles to the West.

It is 5 am. I have been up for three hours, making sure everything is ready. Lizzie was still up when I came downstairs. I had to claim I couldn't sleep. She went to bed at about half two. She always stays up late and then gets up late. We see each other for about eight hours a day when she coincides with my seven am to ten pm schedule. Hers is more two until two.

She made the mistake the other day of getting up at nine and then realised that just meant five more hours of how to occupy yourself during lockdown.

Well, if this works, she can get back to seeing her friends. I wonder whether I should tell her, but Ian and I agreed that involving others might interfere somehow and it is a laughable idea anyway!

159

Ian had the idea, a couple of days after the Premier League decision.

"*Dad. Something weird happened.*"

"*Weirder than Corona virus?*"

"*Yes.*"

"*Good weird or bad weird.*"

"*I am not sure. Do you know how to use Susie's Oculus Rift?*"

Susie had bought herself a lockdown VR present and spent most afternoons crashing our home Wi-Fi by playing Zombies with Jake.

"*I used it once, to look at Macchu Pichu, but it terrified me because the heights looked real.*"

They did. I spent about a minute on it and had already wanted to jump off. Susie says she plays a climbing game wherein falling off feels like the real thing. Not for me.

Ian tells me how to switch it on and how to adjust the straps to fit my larger head.

And he tells me what he has found. And then he shows me. He had been simulating the end of the season on the Rift, to see whether the League got it right. Too much time on his hands, like all of us, but he had coded some algorithm which, according to him, learnt more each time the season was simulated.

Watford rarely got relegated in those simulations, i.e. the Premier League had got it wrong. After an all-nighter of simulating, just out of curiosity, he fed it in a different way around.

What would need to be the case for Watford to stay up?

Disappointingly, but logically when we thought about it, the Corona virus had to have not happened. He had played *around with that and that is when he had found it. He was showing it to me now.*

How the virus had started. The lead scientist had gone home early, and the team had broken the centrifuge machine with the bat blood in it… They cleaned it up as best they could, but Chang went home that night with some on his trainers.

The rest as they say, is, or was, history.

"That's brilliant," I said, "you could market it as a game."

"No Dad, that's not the point. I think I can see back in time."

"Don't talk bollocks. It can't be real. It's just another clever simulation."

"That's what I thought too but I looked up the Chinese scientist in the scenario. She is called Shi Zhengi, and she really exists. She is a virologist in Wuhan, where the virus started."

Well, it took a while. A whole week to be clear. Partly because Susie wanted her Rift back but more because something like this is hard to take in. Partly because I had to join endless Zoom calls about what the world would look like after the virus.

It was not going to be good any time soon.

11 November 2019, or 6 May 2020 (don't ask, neither of us know which day it is).

"It's ringing."
"I know!"
Someone answers.
"Hello," someone answers. It's a man, presumably Yi, her husband.
This is the second time we have called. The first time we realised the flaw (like there was only one!), we didn't speak

161

Mandarin.

But the internet came to our rescue, with some very clever, and very expensive version of Google Translate, we worked out how to make ourselves understood and how to understand Shi and her husband.

It took them a lot longer than it took me to get on board with the idea. We were on the phone on and off for three weeks. Each day waiting for a knock at the door and a man from MI5 to ask us to accompany him to the station.

We showed Shi the footage of the Wuhan lockdown and she actually looked at what happened to her colleagues and her friends.

Susie took her Rift back permanently, so I ordered my own. That took ten days to arrive.

Shi didn't't leave early, even though she did feel unwell. The centrifuge, properly supervised, remained intact.

Ian and I met up at Vicarage Road for the Manchester City home game. Unsurprisingly, we lost, but not six nil this time. We still need a point to be safe

17 May 2020 (again, or a new one?)

………Leno saves it.
The final whistle goes.
We are out of the premiership.
I look at Ian. He is crying.
We stand and hug.

"Which of us is calling Deeney and telling him to hit it to the right?"
"I will."
"I'll get you his number when I get home."
"Ok, love you."
"Love you too."

In the absence of time travel, Watford were relegated from the premiership. My early hope about the end of April turned out to be massively over optimistic and people kept dying, losing their jobs, businesses and savings for the rest of the year and beyond. And Brexit was not cancelled.

PART FOUR – AFTERLIFE

2021 to 2040

Somehow, despite my years of smoking, I avoided the Coronavirus. So did my nearest and dearest, although that is not true for many. And the world feels like it may have changed.

Having spent so much time at home with Lizzie, and survived/enjoyed it, I thought I should retire.

11 October 2021

"I wanted to start by thanking you all for coming."

"I have been to many retirement dos in my time with the firm and it seems to me that they can be quite sad affairs. So I decided I wouldn't have one myself. But then you lot, and you know who you are, put pressure on me, telling me how much you wanted to celebrate my retirement! So maybe it's just sad for the one retiring, and the rest of you can have fun, and a few free drinks."

"Come to think of it that's why you wanted me to put on this event. Well… just to test whether that's the truth, I have decided to ignore tradition and make it a pay bar. So anyone who just came along for a free drink at my expense can leave now."

"My wife, Lizzie, warned me when I tried those lines on her that half of you might leave, so, before that happens, I am joking. There is a free bar and it's scheduled to open at six thirty, so you only have to stand through this thirty-minute presentation and then you can avail yourself of a drink."

"Again, I am joking, it's open now, despite Angus thinking that six is too early to start you lot off drinking, so please help yourselves. I will be brief."

164

"So, as I said, thank you for coming. Those of you who know me will know that I am acknowledged for three things – hopefully more – but definitely three – humour, directness, and my dress sense. Let me deal with each in turn and, perhaps, encourage some of you to pick up the baton going forward. Although in the case of Mike Jones, he has already picked up the baton and is running and out of sight on the dodgy dress sense!"

Mike looks uncomfortable but everyone else gets the joke. He does dress awfully.

"First then, my sense of humour - I think I am funny. I even think the opening piece of this speech is funny, don't you? Not huge laugh out loud funny, I would reserve that for my 'Judgement Day' song at the away day, but alright. I asked my team whether they thought I was funny. They all did, or they all said they did, or Jeff said I was, anyway. It does seem an arbitrary way to hand out bonuses, but I have recommended Jeff for one. To be fair, he has never had one before, so it's probably about time – there I go you see, being funny, or trying to, at Jeff's expense."

Jeff looks less uncomfortable and laughs with the rest.

"The real trick if you want to be funny is that it either has to be at your expense, although not in a way that undermines you, or it has to be done with warmth towards another subject. I hope that, on occasion, or mainly, I have achieved this while at the firm, and I commend it to you."

"That brings me to my second attribute – directness, or some would say earnestness. Others might say "He talks bollocks without thinking about the consequences." I always think about the consequences, but I also think about the impact of not saying what I think, on my self-esteem and you, my colleagues. I used to not think about the consequences. I thought you were supposed to say what you thought. As my career slowed unexpectedly, so I realised that, in some circumstances, you should only say what you thought if it was leadership thought. When I was asked for my opinion, I should have said, "I agree wholeheartedly" more often. But you need to get the balance right."

"Last year was a weird year for us all. And some of us lost loved ones. It was also a weird work year. We had to let some of our colleagues go and the rest of us had to adjust to reduced pay and less contact with each other and our clients. That is behind us now hopefully but, for me, it made me realise that I have done the work phase of my life. That and the fact that I couldn't adjust to not being able to print out my emails and read them. I think we did a much better than many other firms during the crisis. We were largely straightforward with each other. And I hope that continues. It will be real strength for you all as you rebuild.

"So, let me say a few direct, or earnest things about Allens. I love Allens. It gave me a real chance that I didn't expect and you, my colleagues, the leadership and clients have enriched my life. If you cut me, I would bleed our corporate blue. So I care about what happens to you while I am lying on the beach, and not just because you owe me a pension!"

"I have seen lot of change in the years I have worked here. Everyone has got younger for a start, and taller, and better looking, other than you Bill. I think there is lots of change to come. How you respond to that will determine whether we are as successful over the next ten, twenty or forty years, as we have been over the past. Some of that will need to be tactical, as opportunities and threats emerge. Some of it should be directed by us, where we take a lead. In either case it is our culture and how that evolves that is the most important thing."

"We need to remember that our success is as firm, as a team, with our colleagues, not as wilful individuals. We should ask ourselves, and our clients, what they want, not what can we sell them. I know we all understand the difference between helping a client to the right resolution and just telling them, 'Yours is the most hopeless case I have ever seen,' although it might have been better to tell Charlie Fisher that! Only joking Charlie, thanks for coming along, and for forgiving me for getting you one pound in damages."

Charlie nods in my direction and smiles.

"We should price fairly, for the long term. We need to continue to be relevant to smart people but to do that we need to listen to them rather than assume they will want to do it our way. We need to recognise that diversity, in all its forms, is an asset and an obligation, not just what we want to say in our annual report. We need to recognise that our profession and firm are lucky to do the jobs we do, with the rewards, and put something back into the society we live with."

"I know you all know all this, but it merited saying. I wanted to say it, more than telling another joke about Harold's wig. Harold, let me not dwell on your dress sense, but turn to my own. My sense of style was brought to my attention for the first time by Dev, my manager at the time. Thanks for coming Dev, nice to see you. Anyway, it was my appraisal and Dev had been asked to mention my dress sense. In particular my coat and my shoes. Thanks Dev, very helpful. Even less helpful when he posted a note on the coffee machine saying, "Vacancy open – personal dresser for Joe Sandpiper, 'no experience necessary' and everyone says you had no sense of humour!"

"Well, eventually I found a dresser, and much more, my lovely wife Lizzie. Lizzie has steadfastly tried to make me look like the world class professional I am. It is not her fault that I wear everything like it doesn't fit and I never hang my suits up. Even when I clean my shoes so that I can see my face in them, I then insist on stepping in a puddle."

"I have a theory – it's for the benefit of the rest of you. Imagine if I was not only the smartest person in the firm and the best looking but also the best dressed, that would give the rest of you a mountain to climb. I see it as self-sacrifice. I have always said that there are two ways of dealing with most things – be good at them, or dress like you are. I went for the former."

"I shall adopt a different strategy in future, when on the golf course or tennis court, I will be there in the proper kit, in an attempt to look like I know what I am doing. At least until a ball needs striking. I will enjoy it though and, while I will miss Allens, I am going to enjoy even more spending time with Lizzie and the kids and, no pressure, Ian, Susie, the grandkids."

"Thanks very much. Let's all have a drink."

Angus's speech in reply wasn't as funny as mine but then again he hadn't got to be CEO through being a popular. He was very kind about Lizzie though, which I appreciated.

6 July 2022

"Really," says Laura, "You're wearing that?"

I have turned up at her house dressed in a pair of lederhosen Lizzie had bought me in Munich several years ago. I have never worn them, until now.

"I always feel like everyone else is dressed up and I just come in jeans and a T shirt. I thought I'd make the effort."

"Fair enough," she laughs, "but you might have to march far away from us!"

We are going to Pride. We have to be at the start by noon. I am an honorary member of Laura and Zoe's 'Sisters of Music Chapter' – is that what they call it, a Chapter?

I always try to go to Pride if I can. We are definitely now amongst the older participants although, to be fair, Laura and Zoe still look amazing for their age, whereas I am carrying each of my sixty years. Me in lederhosen isn't going to be a good look (and it won't please German men that I think lederhosen are gay in some way) but since I am not trying to impress the women – or not in that way at least – it seems

168

appropriate. Lizzie and Susie have been on the march before with us but not this year.

Zoe appears, looking glamorous in orange and green.

"Hi, how are you?"

We hug.

"How are the kids?"

"Fine."

Laura comes back downstairs, having changed into what looks, to me, like a giant silver bee outfit. Apparently, she wore it once for a weird contemporary / classical fusion concert in Vienna. I admit that I have never seen a silver bee, and that it throws my lederhosen into the shade, and we set off.

The mistake I have made in dressing up for Pride is, of course, to forget about the journey to the event itself. It is one thing, and understandable, to be with the other thousands of marchers, all dressed in the colours of the rainbow and the costumes of the entire animal and plant kingdom. (I know there's a technical term for that –like the periodic table in chemistry - but in biology, but I can't remember it). It's another thing to have to get the number 46 bus from Hackney to Baker Street when most of the other passengers are going shopping.

At least with Pride, it's big and well known enough that you are likely to benefit from a few other marchers being on the bus (there are, including a flower shaped man for Laura's silver bee), and most of the other passengers being aware of Pride. And, by 2022, most of them being relaxed about LGBT.

It was very different twenty or more years ago. After a few drinks Laura will recount the spite and abuse that she and her friends used to get, not just on Pride and similar marches but if they held hands or kissed in public. Even now, not everyone is comfortable and can get their head round the "T" or Trans of LGBT, or the new letter Q. To be honest I don't know what that one means, and I am not sure where I stand on discussions of non-binary and your gender being about what's in your head not between your legs. As a cis straight middle aged white man, all I know is that I am ultra-privileged and that I should try to be gender selection blind. I will have to ask Susie about it.

I don't mind people thinking I don't do all I could to save the planet, but they must not think that I am any sort of "ist".

11 February 2023

I never order first when we go out for a meal. Lizzie usually can't make up her mind, so I have to order one of her two choices. That way she can change her mind once the meals arrive. I don't mind, I am not really into food that much so ending up with her second choice is no hardship. It usually means I end up with the fish dish as she thinks she like fish, or that she should eat it, but she is really a carnivore. If she does have the fish though that's fine with me, so long as her other choice isn't lamb. While the smell no longer takes me back to my time in the abattoir, I don't really like lamb.

Tonight, though I am having fish – sole – while Lizzie has the roast pork, with crackling! I like crackling. Maybe she will share it? We are at one of our regular haunts – I think I have had the sole here before – but at their late sitting. We have been to our solicitors to discuss finally doing our will. It was Lizzie's suggestion that we go out after, which is nice. We haven't been out on our own for a while.

We continue the conversation that we started in the cab from the lawyers – do we want to spend our money or leave it for the kids. Lizzie wants to give it to the kids. I want to spend it, else why have we (I) worked so hard to make it? I don't not want to give anything to Ian and Susie, I just want to have something for us. It isn't like we have a lot of money anyway, but we are entitled to something more than a subsistence living, aren't we?

We are in our sixties and maybe we have got twenty more years?

Which was the remark that kicked the discussion off, I wonder, not for the first time? Although, with hindsight, it's not as simple as one remark or another, or any of these debates in isolation.

"What do you want to do for the next ten years?" she asks.

"Stay alive." It is my standard response.

"And if you do that?"

"Be happy."

"What will make you happy?'

"The kids, the grandchildren, long walks, great holidays, a new car."

"What about me?"

"Yes, what will make you happy?"

"No: am I in your being happy plans?"

"Of course."

"Why?"

"Because. Because I love you."

"Do you?"

"Yes."

"Really?"

"Yes."

"So, what does loving me mean to you?"

I have been here before, many times, it means doing what she wants. No, more than that; it means wanting to do what she wants. I am not going to fall into that trap.

"It means I want you to be happy too."

"And what if we want different things? What if my happy and your happy don't coincide?"

"We'll work it out."

"Go on then, work it out."

171

This is tougher than usual. When is the food going to get here?

"Why don't each of us write down a list of the things we want to do, and then we can choose ones from each list?"

I have tried this technique before, with little success. Lizzie tends to say she is unhappy, without really specifying what she is unhappy about, other than a generic me. So if I can get her to describe what will make her happy then I can try and demonstrably address the list.

It isn't necessarily a risk-free strategy. There have been challenging tasks on previous lists. I have over the years compiled the toughest ten:

1. *Stop flirting with my friends – I don't, flirt with them I mean, but....*
2. *Tell your Mum to stop being horrible to me behind your back*
3. *Get Ian a job*
4. *Stop watching porn – I don't watch it, much*
5. *Stop getting your health checked*
6. *Stop drinking – she never had stop smoking on the list*
7. *You should go and see your dad more often*
8. *Stop arguing with your bosses - no longer an issue after my retirement*
9. *Stop arguing with me*
10. *Let me and the kids argue, it's how we discuss things*

Lizzie has long since worked out that listing is evasion, or at least deferral, on my part. She isn't going to let that go tonight.

"Do you think we have been happy since you retired?"

"We've been OK?"

"I haven't."

"Why?"

"I think you don't make any effort with us. You are

172

great with Ian and Susie and the grandkids and make a real effort. When they are round, we are a family, when they are not, it's like living with a friend, not a lover."

"You mean the sex."

"No, although we could talk about that. No, I mean, there should be love between us not just the occasional TV programme we both enjoy. You should want to be with me, enjoy my company. We are turning into your Mum and Dad. Where eventually we won't even like each other, maybe we'll even dislike each other. I don't want that."

"Nor me."

"So...

Where's the food, it should be here by now...

5 October 2023

We are having an angry row. It is about Ian's plan to move to China. Lizzie said I should tell Ian not to go, or she would. I thought it would be better to be supportive and, if not, I wasn't sure that Lizzie shouting at Ian would be the best way to influence him. Or to leave things if he and Ling actually did move to China. I said as much.

In my head, I only ever speak my mind when I genuinely believe that I am making a constructive contribution. And I am constantly surprised when it is not well received. This isn't just the case with Lizzie, it used to happen at work a lot, and even with the kids. It meant lots of apologising, just to get people back on board, but I have never learnt to 'button it'.

I am fine with this, I think, although I wish I hadn't fought Ian's corner that day (that's how I see it – and then Ian changed his mind anyway!). Would it have made any difference? How many times had Lizzie told me that I was not helping or was undermining her with the kids or others?

We have fought like this before, many times in fact.

Again, in my head, I think of it as a healthy aspect of our relationship, that we can express our views strongly with each other. I love how strong she is in her convictions and, if I am honest, I have often relied upon her drive to get things done or help me feel better. Somehow, though, I cannot square this with her asking me to be more supportive. I feel like I should say what I think and that she should be able to take it on board. I don't need her to agree that I am right, but I do think she should accept that there are alternative points of view to hers.

She isn't my Mum, we are equals. I have seen, in the long run, the damage it did to Dad to always be undermined or forced to be silent when he clearly thought differently from Mum. I am not going to let that happen to me. Like Dad clearly loved Mum, I adore Lizzie, but I do not want to be scared of her.

I have not always felt like this. When we first got together it had been amazing. She had been so sweet to me, and we had lots of amazing times and I was happy to just go along with stuff. Maybe it was when Ian and Susie arrived? I was no longer the centre of her universe, they were. And to be fair, they became the centre of mine too. That there were more conference calls than Elvis and Presley stories when they were growing up was part of providing for them and Lizzie.

I don't want Ian to go to China either. I will really miss him. I already feel sad enough that I do not see enough of Ian and Susie, they have their own lives, so Ian moving thousands of miles away would be terrible. Why don't I say that to Lizzie? Why be stoic instead and try and defend Ian's right to go and, even worse, why criticise her for feeling strongly about it?

**

Lizzie looks up at me. She is wearing an angry face now.

174

"If Ian goes to China. I'm going with him," she says.

"We could do that," I say, unconvincingly.

"Not us, me. Maybe I should go anyway."

She doesn't usually talk like this. She has never talked about her leaving. She has told me to move out a few times before, when our rows got really angry. I had only once thought she had meant it and spent a couple of nights with Laura and Zoe, before coming home.

"So, is that your way of trying to win this argument?" I ask.

"No, I guess it's my way of saying I am tired of arguing with you."

"Ok, let's stop."

"For today, or for good?"

"For today. Or, of course, for as long as possible."

"How long will that be?"

"I don't know."

'That's the problem. I don't know when you are going to be horrible to me again."

"I don't think I am being horrible. Just saying what I think."

'Do you love me?"

"Yes."

"And I love you too, but you do my head in."

This is not going well. Her words are strangely dispassionate. She looks angry but sounds sad.

"What are you saying?" I ask.

"That I am tired of being made to feel bad about what I think."

"I don't mean to do that."

"Maybe you don't but that's what happens."

"I'm sorry."

"For what."

"That I make you feel like that."

175

"So why do you do it?"

"I don't mean to. I was just expressing a view about Ian going to China."

"No, you weren't, you were expressing a negative view about my views on Ian going to China. How did you used to feel at work when people criticised your point of view all the time?"

"They didn't. Sometimes they expressed a different view, but we debated it through."

"Did you always win?"

"Usually."

"There you go. I never win. I am tired of the fight; I want it to stop."

"We don't fight all the time."

"We fight a lot though."

"Do you think we fight more than other middle-aged couples?"

"I don't know, I don't care. If we can't stop fighting we should stop trying to stay together. And we should do it now, before we start hating each other."

"I will never hate you."

"Let's keep it that way."

I want to say that I will hate her if she leaves me but that is too high risk, I might not be able to come back from that. Instead I get her to agree that no one is leaving tonight and that we should go and see a couples' therapist to work on things.

Let's see how that goes. We promised to stay together for richer, for poorer, in sickness and health, until death do us part. Not until one of our children moved to China.

17 March 2024

"I was sorry to hear about you and Lizzie," says Zoe. We have gone for a drink while Laura is away in the US

176

performing.

"Yes, I think I knew it was going to happen, once the kids had left home. Then when I retired so I was at home all day..." I falter.

"Let's see if I can find you a nice straight friend of mine!"

"I'm fine, thanks," I say, although I am anything but.

It is true that it has not come as a real surprise. Lizzie has been telling me for a while that she is not happy with me. I thought that, once I had retired I could spend all my time looking after her and making her feel loved. In my head, the efforts at work were what distracted me from being a great husband. So, when work was done I could be 100% dedicated to this woman that I had chased for years and been married to for nearly thirty. I said as much to her. And while Ian and Susie and my Dad were there at home still, there had been things to do and ways to express my support. Once they had all gone, we struggled, if I am honest. Lizzie said she didn't need a new child at home to look after. And she said it to our therapist!

We went to see two couple therapists. Not pairs of therapists, two at the same time, no, therapists who worked with a couple like us. But maybe that would be a better model, seeing a couple of them? We had started with a man, but Lizzie said he took my side, so we had moved to a woman, Janet. Janet said she saw lots of couples in our situation – they fell in love with each other, then the woman fell in love with the kids and the man fell in love with his work and then when the kids and work had gone, they had to try and fall in love all over again. What had brought us close in the first place? We should try to rediscover that.

I was not happy with the implication that I did not love Ian and Susie too. Janet said that was not what she meant, but I felt that Lizzie should have been quicker to disagree with her too.

177

What was it about me that Lizzie had loved when we got married? I was a decent person apparently, and clever and funny. No, not sexy, although sex had been good, yes. It had pretty much stopped though.

It had been good, I thought, although Lizzie would know better than me. My track record consisted of Jo and two one-night girlfriends (are they girlfriends if it's just one night?) in London in the dozen years before Lizzie and I got together. So, for me, our sex life was amazing and the thing that made me putty in her hands – if that's not a contradiction in terms! "Sexy" was a huge part of it, but not the only reason I loved Lizzie. She was the mother of my children; she was the strong and confident leader of our family and supporter of me.

What's in for Lizzie though? If she just gets a needy friend, and the chance to be part of a family of four? Well now each of us will be a family of one – no that's just me feeling sorry for myself – Ian and Susie are not happy that we were separating but they are old enough to make time for both of us - but I can't help feeling that part of me is missing and, other than getting her back, there will be no way to fill it.

When Ian and Ling did not move to China, I moved in with them and their new twins Zack and Annie. It was lovely but a bit of an imposition on them, as they already had Ling's parents, who moved over from China post Corona. So, in 2025, I made the move. Back home, to Wales.

12 January 2026

Lizzie and I used to go to the cinema quite a lot. Lizzie went to the theatre quite a lot. She usually went with a friend, as I don't really 'get' the theatre. I will go if someone famous is appearing or there is a nice meal to be had. Lizzie is the same with football, if there is food, or Pele or someone like that is

178

playing then she will come. Lizzie's Watford versus Rotherham in the rain is my Waiting for Godot at the National.

Since we split up, though, I went to the theatre with her more often while I was still in London. This is my first trip down from Wales. Today is a Shakespeare matinee. I get Shakespeare, at least it isn't pretending to be real. I can still remember a quote from my school study of Julius Caesar.

"Why man, he doth bestride the narrow world like a Colossus. And we petty men walk under his huge legs, and peep about, to find ourselves dishonourable graves."

Is there something about my relationship with other men in that? Am I a petty one wanting to be a Colossus? I am reading too much into it but there must be a reason I have remembered it.

The Colossus had been on Rhodes and that had been where Lizzie and I had gone on our first holiday post our Cuba honeymoon. We hired a jeep, drove around the island, loving it, and each other, and stopped every hour or so for Lizzie to throw up as she started to ferment the pregnancy that would produce Ian.

We meet on the Southbank before the show. Lizzie looks really well, and I say so. She, Susie and Susie's boyfriend – Jake, he is in advertising - have been to New York for a long weekend. I am not going to get into where she got the money from. She had now got the house, but I am making no payments to her so how she spent her (our) money is her affair.

Talking of affairs, Ian had mentioned that he had been out for dinner with Mum and a guy called Jeremy. Ian said he seemed to be quite well established, although Lizzie had never mentioned him. Not that it could be an affair, we are separated, although we have not got divorced. We presumably now have a very open marriage.

"You look lovely," I say.

'Thanks."

179

"How was New York?"

"You know I love it and it was nice to spend time with Susie. Jake's nice too and she really loves him, which is sweet."

"Just the three of you?'

"Yes, why?" she asks.

"I wondered whether Jeremy would go with you."

"Jeremy?"

"Ian said he met him, you two seemed close."

"He's a good friend, I guess we might go away together but not with the kids, that wouldn't be fair on them."

"What about me?"

"Come on Joe, you know the answer to that. We're not together anymore."

"But I wish we were."

I always do this, every time we meet, push her into saying she doesn't want us to be together. I don't expect any other answer and I am not having a go at her. It just enables me to feel sorry for myself, or hurt. It is like picking at a scab, provoking her until I bleed.

We sit in the silence while the food comes. I play with mine. "Who's in the play," I ask, leaving the scab alone. This is always my role. She allows it, I have responsibility for changing the subject. Although when we were together the subject could not be changed until I had apologised, or the scab was bleeding too much.

"No one you will have heard of, but it's supposed to be really good production. Difficult to get tickets, not the same to see it broadcast live at a cinema."

I would like a beer, even though it is only lunchtime, but I try not to drink when out with Lizzie. It is one of the scabs we have often picked at, that I drink too much. She is much more interested in me stopping drinking than she had ever been in my smoking. I tried to give up smoking during the Corona scare, but failed, and I have never tried to stop drinking

180

although I usually try to moderate it. I was worried that when I moved out, I would be able to start drinking far too much again. So far, I have avoided that and the place I have moved into makes me feel like there is no need, most of the time.

"How's Penarth?"

"It's great, I am much happier there than I was in that hotel, or at Ian's – I was just a burden on him, Ling, and the grandkids. It's full of people older than me, so I feel young and the flats are just across the road from the sea."

"Sounds lovely."

"It is."

And I do think it is, even if my friends and Ian and Susie think it's weird. The kids say that they do understand my need to respond to the double whammy of retirement and then losing Lizzie. But to retreat to Wales and hang out with other sixty somethings, and older, in sheltered accommodation is, I concede, a bit weird. Most of my neighbours are at least ten or fifteen years older. But I like it. I do not know what Lizzie really thinks of it. If she thinks it's not good for me then maybe she should suggest that I come back to live with her?

I enjoy the play – Susie had been in a school production of the same play, so the story is vaguely familiar, and the language pretty digestible, for Shakespeare. Lizzie enjoys it too. I can tell, as I spend as much time watching her as watching the actors on stage.

I take the opportunity to ask her to close her eyes during the love potion moment.

"Open them now," I say and look straight at her.

"You have to fall in love with the first thing you see after you open them."

"I have already fallen in love with you."

"And out though."

"No, just out of love with spending all my time with you."

"It's the same thing," I say, picking away.

4 May 2028

Matilda moved into the Esplanade a year ago, on her own, in the flat next to mine. Many of the other residents are couples, attracted by the location and communal living. It can get lonely, even if there are still the two of you, once the kids have left home. Dave and I are two of only four single men. Dave is definitely single, his wife died a few years ago. I am, temporarily at least, as Lizzie stubbornly refused to move from London and has, in fact recently gone on holiday with that Jeremy chap. Why do I say chap, I mean something much ruder, another four letter 'c' word.

Matilda, like me, is separated, although in her case divorced and she has never had any children. She had been an English teacher in Pembrokeshire and also a poet. Her poetry is invariably upbeat and cheerful, unlike my teenage efforts. She says she is impressed with some of my work, although more, I suspect, with the fact that I had kept it all these years. With her help, I have turned my hand to poetry once again, and she is teaching me about iambic pentameter, and all those clever proper poetry rules.

My newer stuff is better poetry and a different tone from before. In 1977, I had written a Poem called, "Fuck Off!"

No one really
Wants to know
If I am Ok
Doesn't mean
They'll be your friend tomorrow
Just 'cos they're nice today
I'm only out
To get what I can

I'll only love you
When I need you man

If I wanna hit someone
Stay outta my way
If I need to be violent
Don't matter what you say

Drink too much
Smoke a lot and screw
No one's gonna
Care too much for you

You've gotta be nasty
To get on
Do anything for nothing
You won't last too long

If I ever get anywhere
Then I'll laugh
It always looks better
If you're the other half

We all know
Everyone else is a shit
Not to put
Too fine a point on it

At least it rhymes but I am not sure where all the 'wanna's and 'gonna's came from. We did try it as lyrics at a Cosmopolitan gig, where it went down OK, and I do like the last verse but it's not a great world view for a seventeen-year-old is it?

183

Fifty years later and I am writing "A Lover's Cove":

Bright is the light, which sweeps the shore
In comes the tide we have been waiting for
Imprints in the sand, a gentle mould
Rough cliffs above reflect gold

Romancing couples drinking wine
The waves break their line
To us a haven for our lover
A mere beach to another

Being the poetic soul I was
Loving the feel of the place, because
I can smell the salt in your hair
And see my happiness there

Memories of my wife wing back
The half of me I nowadays lack
With our children gone and grown
Here, with you, is my home

I am not as content as the poem implies, really, but I think Matilda appreciates this sort of poem. I am happier than I have been for while though, as well as a more technically proficient poet. The latter is thanks to Matilda and, to be fair, so is a bit of the former.

We're not in love, or anything, I am still in love with Lizzie and will be until the day I die. And if she calls and asks me to come home, I will be there in a shot, but she hasn't so far, and life needs to be lived everyday not just postponed for some distant hope.

As well as writing poetry together, Matilda and I go for long walks and we like the same TV programmes. She is also trying to address my literature deficit. I used to read a lot but none of the so-called greats of English literature. I had never read Austen, or the Brontes or Chaucer, Eliot or even some of the modern ones like Rushdie. I am not sure all of them are that great, now having read them, but what do I know?

Matilda and I take on Rose and Dave in my version of bridge. Matilda and I always win, and it partly offsets Dave's persistent chess victories over me.

1 June 2028

"What are you going to say at the wedding, Dad?" Susie asks me a couple of weeks before the event.

"Why, are you worried?"

"No, although please don't go on about you and mum having split up."

"Is she bringing Jeremy?"

"You know she is."

"How old is he?"

"Fifty, I think."

"And he's been married before?"

"Yes, you know that. He's really nice to Mum. Are you bringing anyone?"

"Matilda asked whether she could come."

"You should bring her."

"I know, but I don't want Mum to think I brought Matilda to make a point, or to show that I am happy without her."

"Are you, though?"

"Not as happy as I would be with her."

'Yes, but that's not going to happen, bring Matilda if she makes you happy."

'Maybe, anyway, it's not about whether I am happy, it's about you being happy."

"I am always, or almost always, happy Dad, you know that. You and Mum being happy is important to me too."

"How's work?"

"It's great at the moment. We have a huge fundraising coming up. I half tried to persuade Jake to postpone the honeymoon, but he rightly said we'd never go if we don't go now."

"I think it's really cool that you guys are going to Cuba."

"You and Mum talk, or talked about, it so much I always wanted to go, although I think it's very different now from when you went."

"No more Castro, and full of Americans."

"USA citizens."

"Sorry yes, I am forgetting my political correctness lessons, being in the wilds of Wales."

"That's no excuse, you were always right on."

"I like to think so, and that I am still but if I am honest, I do have to work at it, not like you."

"It's a different age now, plus you and Mum always brought Ian and me up to have the right attitudes. Although I agree you think it's cool to have a gay older sister, while I just think Laura is cool."

"She wasn't always gay you know."

"Really?"

"Well, you know what I mean, she went out with boys in her twenties."

"Well, I went out with girls in my twenties."

"Really."

"No, actually, but lots of my friends did."

"As you say, it's a different age."

"I think, you must know this, Laura was probably always gay, and knew she was but it must have been much tougher for people to come out then. Maybe that's why she left it so late. She and Zoe were always the coolest couple though, so I think she made up for it."

"I guess."

"Why don't you like talking about this?"

"I think about how sad it is that they haven't had any children."

"That's a choice, not because they are gay."

"Yes, but I suppose I assume that they thought it would be more difficult to have kids and explain the whole two mums' thing."

"You should ask her. I just think they did not want to have children."

"I can't understand that though, having your own kids is the greatest thing you can ever do. I am prouder of you and Ian than anything else in the world. I love you beyond reason."

"Dad, I know you love me and Ian, you have kept telling us, and making it clear you do. I have told you lots of times that you should have saved some of that love, or expressing it, for Mum and, importantly, yourself."

"I know, I remember that poem you wrote me for my fiftieth. I still have it."

Half life

A glass bottle washes up on a lime green shore
Empty; disappointingly cliché-less.
A metaphor for life?

Joy has not been neatly parcelled out as we hoped.
The sun's rays burn and infect our skin.
The air fills with the world's toxic breath.

And, slumped over a brown leather armchair,

187

Hair cascades from your ever-balding head like a waterfall
As your face wrinkles, imprinted by the weight of so many years

Some days are like this.
Some days you are blind.
Some days you feel alone.

Yet you have made it -
Fifty years is fifty years more than some
And you, as I do, should look forward to the same again

Because they will be filled with joy
And sunshine that illuminates your spirit
And air that only seeks to refresh your mind.

If you allow yourself the strength to sit up straight
And never have too much pride,
You will see that these wrinkles are trophies of time:

One for your selfless work ethic,
One for the eternal love of your family,
And the rest for a struggle that we all know,
The fight to find, and love, yourself.

I love you Dad,
Now, always,
Round the back and infinity.

15 June 2028

"You are cordially invited to the wedding of Susie Sandpiper and Jake South at St Catherine's Church, N10, at 3 pm and afterwards at 7 pm at Alexandra Palace on Saturday 15 June 2028. RSVP"

I have been looking forward this day for months and, as Matilda and others have pointed out, talked about very little else. Now it is time for my speech.

I clink my glass with a spoon, cough and stand.

"Sorry to interrupt the conversation. You all sound like you are having a great time, but I want to say a few words."

People look at me.

"I am very lucky, in all sorts of ways, to be able to say a few words at one of the best days in my family's life. One of the ways I am lucky is that, apparently, according to Susie and Jake, it is no longer trendy for the father of the bride to make a speech. It's very old fashioned, like Susie can't speak for herself. I agree, so I am not going to make a speech."

And I sit down.

"Dad," laughs Susie, 'some people will think you mean it!"

I stand up.

"Just one of my moments of inappropriate humour. In truth Susie and Lizzie asked me whether I would say something, and I am really happy to be asked. What I should say now is how I looked up Father of the Bride speeches on the internet to find the best jokes and things to say. But I didn't do that. You would hope that when your daughter gets married you have something in your head which you want to say, and that people want to hear. I hope I do."

"One of the things Susie knows I often do on such occasions is write a poem. Sometimes a proper one, sometimes less so. My default is something that doesn't rhyme and doesn't scan but is a sort of initials led verse. Apparently, it's called an acrostic."

"Susie and Jake, I am sure you'll be delighted to hear I have one for this event. It's called, obviously, 'Woman and Husband'. A little bit of gender politics reversal for you there.'

When you were born (W you see)
Output of our love (O)
Maybe we thought you would
Add to our happiness
No, you have done so much more than that

And even more so today
Now I know you know but one can never say it too much
Dad and Mum love their daughter

He's not bad too
Understands how to look after
Susie and
Because she loves him, we do too
And his family, welcome to ours
Now, just to repeat myself
Dad and Mum love their daughter and, Ian, their son too."

"We remember when Lizzie was first pregnant, with Ian, how excited we were both were, when she wasn't throwing up, about having children. Nothing has been richer in our lives than seeing Ian and Susie grow up. Ian already has his own family. It's great to see Ling's parents, here. I hope they will forgive me for saying so, it's even more exciting to see Zack and Annie, our first grandchildren. Wherever they are – there you are!"

"Now it's Ian's baby sister's – she hates me calling her that – it's Susie's turn and we couldn't be prouder of her, of the young woman she has grown up to be, of the life she has built and of the man she has chosen to marry today."

"We first met Jake. Sorry, I first met Jake. I keep talking as if Lizzie and I are still together. I think you met him before I did Lizzie. Sorry again, I promised Susie I wouldn't talk about Lizzie and my marriage and recent difficulties, not the right topic for her wedding day. Anyway, I first met Jake a couple of years ago, at his thirtieth birthday party. From that you can work out he's much older than Susie, although men are so much less mature than women, so it makes sense, and its nowhere near the "half you age plus seven" rule, its only two years. Not quite so sure about you and Jeremy on that rule though, Lizzie? Sorry, inappropriate humour again."

"So, Jake and I met at his thirtieth, where I also met Jeff and Paula, his parents, and Penny, his sister. Welcome all of you to our extended family. Jake is an amazing guy and it's clear what Susie sees in him. It's a bit disappointing he's not a Catholic, because I know how seriously Susie takes the religion she inherited from Lizzie and me! Other than that, he seems perfect."

"To be clear, though, he would need to be. Otherwise, he would not be good enough for Susie."

"Everyone, or maybe almost everyone, loves their children, and no parent can be objective about their own kids. But in Susie, and Ian – but it's not your day mate! In Susie I am so lucky to have ended up knowing and being close to one of the best people in the world. There are three women in my life in reality – there were four, but I lost my mum a while ago – and all three of them, Lizzie, Laura and Susie are amazing, and not just for sticking with me or, in Lizzie's case, for trying very hard to."

"If my big sister taught me how wonderful women could be, and my wife taught how to be with them then Susie has shown me how much better they are than I and my generation have been. There is no-one kinder, more tolerant, but passionate about what she believes in. No one who is a better daughter, or sister, or niece, of friend than she is. No one who will make a better daughter in law – Paula, take note - although to be fair she has real competition from Ling, who is an amazing daughter in law. No one who will make a better

191

mum one day – with respect to the other mums here and those we have lost."

"I, we, love, you and Jake with all our heart and wish you the happiest and longest of lives. It has been a real privilege to be your father. And to be here today is one of the best days of my life. It could only be bettered if you had let me show that video of you in the nativity at school, but you vetoed that. If anyone of you want to see it let me know, the bit when she drops the baby Jesus on his head is great, especially as they were using a real baby! A joke, that last bit."

"To Susie, and Jake, the very, very lucky couple."

***

The ceremony itself is beautiful. The sun shines, the choir sing like angels, Laura plays like one, and Susie looks like one. I don't go to church very often, just events like this, but they do them well. The priest is impressive, and she gets the balance right between celebration and service.

Lizzie has always said I should get into religion, certainly as I get older, as a way of mitigating my fear of dying. She also thought that maybe the kids needed to be exposed so that they didn't suddenly go cultish in their twenties. They were both christened but, other than an attempt to get Ian into the local Catholic primary (failed), they did not attend regular church again. Lizzie didn't do religion herself, any legacy of generations of Spanish Catholicism was finally vanquished by her convent experience.

I went to Sunday School as a child, as did Laura, to some weird Welsh sect – Baptists they were called. Our parents didn't go, but the church had been smart enough to put on a coach which collected kids from their heathen parents every Sunday morning, allowing the parents a lie in, and their offspring to learn about the prodigal son and the Ten

Commandments. We also both joined the Boys and Girls Brigades at the church – a sort of weird combination of Scouts/Guides and the Salvation Army. At some stage, at a much later age than Laura, I worked out that it was all too uncool and stopped going. Not because I didn't believe, nor because I didn't enjoy it but just because I didn't want to be seen attending stuff like that.

In fact, I did believe, for quite a while and it was a bitter disappointment to me when I worked out that it wasn't all true. I still hope it might be - hence Lizzie's encouragement – but was quite angry with God when I first realised that he might not exist.

God formed the subject matter of a number of my teenage poetic outbursts.

Crawling on your knees (1978 – more punk lyrics than verse?)

> *I could walk on water*
> *Or cure the lame and dead*
> *Nobody would worship me*
> *No crown of thorns for my head*
>
> *I could crucify myself*
> *They wouldn't glorify my name*
> *Call myself the son of god*
> *Would they believe me?*
> *Like fuck they would*
>
> *We don't need religion*
> *False morality based on fear*
> *Go to church on Sunday*
> *Offer up your prayer*
> *You can sin now*

You're forgiven
By a non-existent god

But when you die
And there's no more
What the fuck was it all for?

Indeed.

***

"Great speech Joe"

"Thanks Jeff. I thought Jake's was brilliant, funny but heartfelt too."

"Susie's was even funnier though. Amazing. Although she is amazing, we're so happy things worked out with Jake and her."

"So we are."

"Penny and Richard are getting married next year. I need to work on my father of the bride speech!"

"Where's the wedding?"

"Just outside Bristol, near where we live. Expect your invitation shortly"

"I look forward to it"

"And you must come and visit Paula and I. Bring your friend, sorry I have forgotten her name."

"Matilda."

"Yes, Matilda, both of you should come down. I'll get Paula to sort it out with you."

I had brought Matilda in the end. I told Lizzie beforehand, and she said it was fine. I explained that she wasn't a girlfriend or anything, not like her and Jeremy, but just some company for the train journeys and a chance for Matilda to meet all these people I kept going about at the home. Of course, not deciding until late on had caused "havoc" with the seating plans. Should she be on the top table, who should she sit next to, if she wasn't coming who got "promoted" from table two?

This is the third wedding that Lizzie has planned, her (our) own, Ian's and now Susie's. No need for a fourth for her and Jeremy! She is really good at it. In fact, she is really good at everything she does. She had been a much better lawyer than me, until she stopped to look after Ian and Susie and my Dad. Certainly, a more successful and popular one, and I think if we had our time again (oh, if only, certainly some bits of it!) then I think it would have been smarter for me to stay at home with the kids and let her career flourish – maybe we would still be together, or, maybe, she would have been off sooner. How would I feel without my career, what would I have done instead – anything – lots of walks, some more poems, learnt to cook and garden?

Jeff goes to get us both a drink. I look around for Matilda. I can see that she is talking to Laura and Zoe –about me? Is that going to go well? I grab my drink from Jeff and go over.

Not being my first drink, I am emboldened and venture "How are we ladies?" as my opening shot.

"Fuck off," says Laura.

"Laura, Matilda is not used to such language!'

"Fuck off," says Matilda

"How's the father of the bride doing?" asks Zoe

"Well, very well."

"Many more of those and you'll be sleeping on the floor!" says Matilda.

"She's joking… we have separate rooms."

"I should hope so, at your age!" says Zoe, "heterosexual sex should stop for good at about fifty."

'Is it different if you are gay then?" I ask.

"Absolutely, if you're gay it is compulsory to have sex into your nineties." says Laura

"There are less of us you see so we each have to have more sex to make up for it," she adds.

"I am going to find the groom for a dance" says Matilda.

"You can dance with me if you like"

"Maybe later" and she goes off.

"See" I say, "You have scared her off with all that talk of sex."

"Not based upon the conversation we were just having!"

"Really?"

"Yes, you should get to know her better, and maybe in that way too, if you still can!"

"Very funny!" (Although probably right.)

"Susie looks amazing" says Zoe, "if I was twenty years younger and she was gay…"

"Actually, she gets it from her mum. If you were ten years younger and Lizzie was gay…"

"And I didn't have Laura." says Zoe, "Did you ever think about being gay?"

This is one of Zoe's standard questions of me, which I never feel quite comfortable about how to answer.

"As you well know, I didn't even know it was an option until I came to London."

I am surprised by how naïve I was when young or unknowing. I had little awareness of homosexuality. Not the same as being actively against but as a young man I will have used my fair share of 'poof' and many other phrases in negative ways. Nothing but harm came from homophobia (and sexism and racism) of the past, and I know that now, and regret not having known it from day one. Maybe if I had been more thoughtful about Laura's sexuality earlier that would have

196

helped.

Now though I am quite good with it, aren't I?

"Laura, why have you and Zoe never got married and never had kids?" I ask.

"Why do you ask?"

"We're at my daughter's wedding, it crops up. Actually, Susie and I were talking about it."

"The wedding bit's easy. We spent so long arguing that we were as valid as a couple regardless of not being allowed to marry that by the time they legalised it we felt it would be a betrayal of that to then get married."

"Not having kids is more complicated. Zoe wanted them and I didn't. I was always travelling for my music and I didn't want her to stay at home as the "mum"."

"We agreed, although I have donated my eggs to IVF for other couples, so there may well be bits of me out there" says Zoe.

"Wow, I never knew that."

"No, now you do."

"So you still haven't answered the "Did you think about being gay question!"

"I know."

One of the best days of my life had to eventually end. We waved Susie and Jake off as they set off to spend, hopefully, the rest of their lives together. I hope Susie lives forever.

Lizzie comes over and stands next to me.

"Matilda's nice."

"So is Jeremy."

'He is, although you don't mean that."

"No, I don't but I imagine he would be if he wasn't with you."

"Are you saying I make him nasty?"

"No, that's not what I meant, I meant I can't help but

197

think him evil as he stole you off me."

'You know that's not true"

"Ok, he's keeping you from me, or me from you anyway."

"Let's not do this now, on our daughter's wedding day. We were a great couple and we have been great parents. We are great friends and will be forever."

"Is that good enough for you?"

"It's more than many, if not most."

"When are you going back?"

"Tomorrow, Matilda and I have a train from Paddington at noon."

"Oh, Jeremy and I are going out for dinner with Jeff and Paula and Ling and her parents tomorrow night. Do you have a flexible ticket? You guys should come."

"Thanks, but no, the tickets aren't flexible and anyway it would probably be a bit much for Matilda, two Sandpiper get-togethers in a row. I realise now I shouldn't have brought her. It's not helped with your and my relationship."

"Oh, Joe, you surely know me better than that, I am happy you have other people in your life. I mean it, she seems nice. What are some of the others like at the care home?" she laughs.

"It's not a care home, it's independent living apartments – like people choosing to hang out together."

"I know you wanted to go back to the sea, but I thought you'd end up in Brighton or somewhere. You are miles from anywhere."

"I always wanted to go back to Wales and be near the sea, but you love London, so it was never going to happen. I might as well get something good out of us not being together."

"Did you not get something good out of us being together – Ian and Susie at least."

"You know I got a lot more than that. I still love you.

198

When that love worked, and we were together, I got everything from you. You gave birth to, and brought up, my two children. You gave up your job and enabled me to get up and go to work every day. You let me share your friends. You picked me up from, or pushed me out of, my mad moments."

She kisses me on the cheek and goes back inside.

***

"How was the wedding?" asks Dave.

"Amazing, lovely, even better than Ian's."

"And how did you and Matilda get on?" he asks, and winks.

"I was the perfect gentleman," I say.

"How disappointing, Jock and I thought there was hope for us all but not if you and Matilda can't get it together!"

"There is more to life than sex, Dave."

"Yes, but sex makes the world go round a lot quicker than all the other stuff, at least if I remember it rightly."

22 February 2030

"What's that?" asks Annie.

"That's a camel. They usually live in the desert. You see that lump on its back. That's where it stores water."

"That one's got two lumps," says Zack, "does it store food in the other lump?"

"I think so."

I love bringing Zack and Annie to the zoo. I have always loved zoos. Not for me the disappointment with the unnatural conditions they live in or the liberation struggles of trapped wild creatures. Put me in a park with fifty varieties of creature and I can while away hours, or days. An enthusiasm I hope to transmit to the little ones. It seems to be working.

199

We are at Whipsnade. Less species but more space that London Zoo and, on a gloriously sunny day like today, no better place. Ling dropped us off and is going to be back at five. She and Ian have an annual pass as they live so near and when she is back she has promised the kids that they can "drive" the car though the deer park. Ian has been away all week in Germany, but I still came down for the week to stay with Ling and the kids for half term.

"Who wants an ice cream?"

Two "Me's."

This will be second of the afternoon, but Ling has not sent us with any sandwiches and the food at Whipsnade is probably no healthier than ice creams so what the hell!

Plus I have taken up ice cream as one of my nicotine substitutes. It is now five years since I had had a cigarette, or certainly since I have been a smoker. There has been the occasional lapse, never more than a couple (how many is a couple, is it always only two?), always drink induced, and never more than a couple of times a year. I have Zack and Annie to thank for me finally quitting. By the time I could no longer run around without coughing, Ian and Susie no longer required me to run around with them, but Zack and Annie expect me to. After one particularly energetic paddling pool playtime I genuinely felt like I was having a heart attack (i.e. it was different from the "many" I had had before) and resolved to stop.

At least it means I get to push them in their chair when they get tired, as opposed to the other way round.

I did ask Lizzie whether she would have me back now I had stopped smoking. She said that if I also stopped drinking she would think about it but as alcohol was another one of my nicotine substitutes that seemed an unrealistic ask. She did congratulate me though – maybe, now, I would live forever, as I wanted.

Zack and Annie probably will live forever. Medicine and genetics have progressed so far that everyone is supposed to live beyond 100 and, for the youngest like them, science would stand a good chance of extending that. I am sure they don't think about it (how worrying would that be, even I didn't start worrying about not existing until I was eighteen) but I do think about it. It makes me excited for them, and a little bit envious.

We will finish our 99s (why were they called that, presumably, they used to cost 99p, now they should be called 500s – apparently its actually to do with the 99 soldiers who guarded the King of Italy, so its special in some way), and go to the butterfly house. If you stand still the butterflies will land on you. Some of them are quite large. Last time we were here I had let them land on the grandchildren. There were none of the hysterics that would have ensued if they had landed on me. They clearly had some healthy additions to the genetic anxiety pool I had endowed them with. Both Lizzie and Ling were the sort of mums who would happily wander the streets with a tarantula on their head. I would have died of fright.

My dad would have caught it, stuck a pin in it and put in a glass box.

Jeremy and Lizzie did get married. I didn't go to the wedding. As if by way of retaliation, I moved in with Matilda.

Lots of other stuff happened although I am starting to forget some of it. Matilda says that we went to Laura's eightieth, to Angel's christening (is that a proper name for a child, Susie?) and on a cruise of the Med and that I enjoyed them all.

2 July 2034

"Come on Sandpiper, the game's on in thirty minutes, I've saved you a chair."

So, for the first time since I was five, England are in the World Cup Final. It is amazing really, no one had expected it. They had only just qualified for the tournament at all and then lost their best player to an injury in the FA Cup Final, but here they were, in the Final! The whole country has ground to a halt and, even here in Wales, there are England flags everywhere.

Ian and his whole family have gone out to China for the tournament, staying with Ling's extended family. They invited Lizzie and me but, at our age it would have been a trip too far. I said to Lizzie that she and Jeremy should go. She said I should go with Ian, but we have stayed at home. If I had expected them to do this well, maybe I would have gone. Although Ian said they didn't have tickets for the final. He had been to the semi-final against Germany though. England winning on penalties, who would have thought it!

The key, we have all now decided, is the manager, Jose Mourinho, ex most of our PL cubs and Portugal, and the foreign player rule introduced in the Premiership in 2022, which gave our best players more first team experience. No one expects us to beat China though; they have been ruthless in every round, despite losing two of their expected tournament stars to doping accusations.

"I'll be there in two minutes."

"Do you want a beer?"

"No thanks, you know I don't drink alcohol before six o clock."

"Even when England are in the World Cup Final? And anyway its eight thirty in the evening in Beijing."

'You make a very good point, yes I'll have one."

Matilda doesn't really like football but even she recognises that this is the World Cup Final and England might win it. I doubt they will though, although I don't really mind. It'll be nice to watch it with Matilda and Dave and the others, and I can always claim to be Chinese via Ian's in laws if the result goes against us.

When I got too infirm, Matilda and I moved into a care home on the Gower. Even further from London but such a beautiful spot. And Dave had moved there a couple of years before.

14 June 2038

We are out in the garden – another sunny day – maybe ten of us. Half of us is playing a rather feeble, but fun, game of cricket. Dave is bowling from his wheelchair – it isn't really fair to ask him to field – and I am the wicket keeper. We are only playing with a tennis ball, so it isn't too hazardous a role.

Matilda is batting or, trying to. It is obvious that she never played cricket properly, as she constantly wants to hit the ball with a rounders' type of swing. Combine that with Dave's less than lethal bowling and the game is clearly going to go on for a while. Matilda scores the occasional bye when I can't reach down quick enough to stop one of Dave's daisy cutters but, other than that, it isn't going to be a high scoring game.

Dave and I run the semi-official sports and games league for my and Matilda's and my new home, Seaside House – for bowls, cricket, darts and board games. The competition runs monthly, and Dave's team had won in both April and May. I need to win in June.

"Matilda, do you want to swap after a few more balls?" I ask.

"OK, just a few more."

203

She hits none of those either, but nor do they trouble the wicket, and we swap. Dave isn't sure this is in accordance with the rules but lets it go after being instructed to do so by the "umpire" – Helen from the staff.

Matilda doesn't want to be wicket keeper, so Mike comes in. That is actually a bit of a problem because, as well as being part of Dave's squad, he is younger and fitter than the rest of us – not a high standard admittedly, but it is all relative.

I take the bat from Matilda and settle myself into the crease – doing that thing where you ask Dave to give you a line and marking it in the turf. I have no idea why I am doing it, but they do it on TV. I study the field, again learnt from Test Match Special – Alice is at long off, I think that's where she is, or she might just be looking at the flowers. Matilda is on the leg side, Mike behind the wicket. You are out if you hit the ball over the fence, so the available shots are limited.

Dave bowls. I swish and miss. Mike catches it and immediately knocks the bails off. "You were out of your crease!" he cries. "Howzat?!" he appeals to Helen.

I look at her. We usually have a rule that you can't be out first ball, but I don't really want to rely on that unless I have to.

"Not Out," she says. Thank goodness for that. Mike puts the bails back on and throws the ball to Dave. "Here comes a fast one." Dave shouts and bowls a full toss at me. I move down the wicket and hit it firmly back at Dave. Even though he is in a wheelchair, I know Dave will have a go at catching it. If I am going to get any runs at all, I need to run before he does so. Usually we don't run, we just walk to the bowler's wicket and then are allowed to walk back for the next ball. But here, I need to get to Dave before the ball, on the off chance he catches it. I don't want to be out for a duck.

Anyway, when you are nearly 80 and you haven't run anywhere for maybe ten years this is not a smart move and, halfway down what is a pretty short pitch, I trip over the bat I am carrying and land on my knee.

Helen takes me to A&E – I sort of recognise it so have probably been here before – just in case. My knee hurts a lot but, as the doctor says, I landed on a lawn not concrete, so it is likely to be just bruised and sore rather than anything worse. Nevertheless, they do an x ray, which means we are there for a while. Nothing is broken but they give me a crutch to hobble home with.

When I finally get back, Dave and I agree that the match should be put down as Abandoned, and that I should be recorded as 1, not out which, given that he caught the ball, is gracious of him.

15 June 2040

"Joseph, time to get up."

Someone is talking to me.

I wonder how long they have been there.

"Time to get up Joe," she says again.

"I am happy here in bed, thanks," I say.

"Yes, but its morning time now and it will be breakfast soon."

"I don't want breakfast."

"Yes, but you have to get up anyway."

"I was having a dream."

She laughs.

"You are always dreaming. But now it's time to get up."

I open my eyes and look at her. I can't remember who she is. She is carrying a glass of water and a small plastic cup with a large blue pill in it.

"Take this before you get up," Matilda says, and heads to the door. I have recognised her.

205

"Breakfast in ten minutes," she says and leaves the room.

I watch her leave, now having forgotten what I was dreaming about. It wasn't a nice dream, I know that, but the moment is gone.

To be fair to Matilda, I am hungry, so the thought of breakfast in ten minutes does motivate me.

Raising my head from the pillow, I look out of the window. The sun is shining. That's good. It means we should be able to be out in the garden, or even go for a short walk - another reason for getting up.

The home - Seaside House I think it's called - is right next one of the nicest beaches in Wales – Rhossili Bay. I once found a website which ranked it as one of the best beaches in the world. It's nice yes and it's in Wales, but in the world? I don't get to use it much, whatever its ranking. The home used to be a hotel and overlooks the bay and an island called Worm's Head. It's really "Wurm" as in the Welsh for dragon, rather than the less glamorous English earthworm (my plan to write some of this in Welsh would have reduced its limited appeal to a number it would be quicker to meet and tell the story to).

The views are spectacular, and the sunsets are lovely (as I assume are the sunrises which I invariably sleep through) but at best we usually end up in the garden or potter to the village pub. It rains much of the time (wettest beach in the world anyone?) and half of us struggle to get out of bed ourselves. So we are not really fit for clambering across the low tide rocks to the Wurm's tail, let alone his (her? What gender is the island? Boats are female, maybe all things on water are?) Head.

It has been raining for a few days, even though I think it is the summer now, so to see the sun out this morning is good. I will get up, although I had better take my tablet first or Matilda will be cross. I can't remember when I started taking

206

the tablets; maybe even before I came to Seaside House. I can't remember that either, when it is that I first came here. I don't know what's in the tablet, but it's designed specifically for me apparently, which is very clever. It's partly for (what is left of) my memory but there are lots of other things in there –for cholesterol, blood pressure, bone strength, mood, sexual function (not a lot of call for that).

I often wonder what will happen if I don't take them. Will I disappear in a puff of smoke or just feel really ill? Probably not worth the risk of finding out, I load the tablet, swallow and wash it down.

I put the cup back down on my bedside table and take a look around my room – I live in room 212, on the second floor. It's not a huge room but it's big enough for me. Apart from the bedside table, there is a wardrobe, a small table and chair, and lots of pictures – of my family presumably – and a large TV on the wall. The TV is silent but has a message on its screen.

"Good morning
Today is 15 June 2040
It is 9.05 am and breakfast is being served
If you need help pull the cord by your bed.
Bethan Davies
Manager
Seaside House"

Room 212 is actually technically two rooms as I have an ensuite bathroom. It doesn't have a bath, but it has a shower and toilet. Off there next.

As I said, I think most of the pictures on the walls are of members of my family. There is one of me and my Mum and Dad. They are dead, I think. Not in the photograph, but in real life. I don't know exactly when they died, but it's a while ago.

My Mum died first and then my Dad ended up in a home for a while. His was not one like this though. His was really just like a dementia waiting room with guards. Seaside House is supposed to be more like a holiday camp, with entertainers, although the average age is about the same as where my Dad was. I think I am a lot happier here than he was at his home. And I am not on my own, Matilda is in the next room

The other main photo on the wall is us - me and my wife, while she was still with me. I remember now, that's why I moved back to Wales and in here, because it was really lonely living on my own, even though I was nearer the kids before I moved. They are somewhere in London.

There are some other people I don't really recognise. I guess it's unlikely that I would have photos of random strangers on the walls of my room so I guess I must have known who they are. I think I have a sister, so presumably she is one of them. The only other pictures I recognise are on my bedside table, the most important pictures, one of my two children. And our family dog – he's dead too, but the kids aren't.

And, according to my diary, also on the bedside table, my son is coming to see me this evening. That will be good, maybe we can go to the pub if he's not here too late.

Looking at the clock, breakfast will have already started downstairs, but they don't mind if you are late; so long as I get there before nine-thirty they will still serve me. Still, I had better get a move on.

Matilda has put out some clothes for me, so now I have taken my tablet I just need to actually get up, go to the loo and put the clothes on. I clamber out of bed. I have to do this gingerly as my left knee is sore from a fall a couple of years ago. I can't remember how I hurt it.

So far, touch wood, I have avoided any serious operations. Matilda has a new knee and Dave is in wheelchair after he broke his hip. I still have all my original bits and pieces and they work well, after a fashion. That's good because if you can't do things yourself then the staff have to help. I am sure they would try hard to put you at your ease but having strangers dress you or put you on the toilet or in the shower must be pretty uncomfortable.

I remember that I once took my Dad away for a few days when he was in his home. Having to wash him and dress him, taking him to the toilet, always too late and wiping him and putting on clean incontinence pants were not my favourite moments. Nor his, I am sure. Changing your child's nappy is part of the natural order of things. The reverse is not. At least for my Dad, when he got to that stage, maybe he didn't really know what was going on or that it was his son, rather than the staff, who were changing him? It's probably better to go mentally and physically at the same time? Although probably even better, at that stage, just to "go"?

I wash and dress myself – 'shower, shit and shave' as they say, in the Army maybe – not that I have done any of those. Pill, cardigan and crutch –not something they would say in the Army, maybe in the Salvation Army? It is time to go down for breakfast.

Sometimes I use the stairs to go down to the ground floor but today, with my crutch, I limp towards, into, and out of the lift. I always use the lift to go up anyway.

I usually sit with Dave and Jock for meals. Ever since his hip operation, Dave has been in a wheelchair – he shows no signs of improving enough to get out of it again – even though he is a bit younger than me. Jock isn't, at least he does not look it – he must be ten years older than me, so that's what age?

They are both at the table already this morning. Matilda is sat at another table chatting with Rose and Alice, so I wave and smile at her and will sit in my old place with the boys. I am usually the last to arrive, and the first to leave. I have been a vegetarian for a while now, but I no longer have to put up with

Dave and Jock's 'But what about the smell of freshly cooked bacon?' challenge to my status. Everyone is a vegetarian these days. Not because they don't want to eat animals but because that's the way the food industry has gone. It isn't because it was inhumane to eat animals, just not efficient or economic enough for the populations that needed feeding. So apparently many foodstuffs are now GM protein and carbohydrates.

The food industry still produces 'meat' dishes as that makes the food seem more palatable, but many fewer people actually get to eat real meat these days. I assume.

Do Dave and Jock know this when they happily tuck into their 'steak and kidney' pie or, this morning's 'bacon' and 'eggs'? Maybe I should tell them just in case? Jock would be really cross, I imagine, if he didn't already know. I will leave it.

I am not sure why I became vegetarian – I haven't always been one. I think that I woke up one morning and decided that I would be one. I know some people do it for health reasons and others for animal welfare. I don't particularly care about animals. We used to have a dog, and I loved him but generally I don't worry about animals. I do remember that there used to be a fad for only eating ones who have a nice life before they get killed and cooked. I could never understand that. Either an animal is a valid thing with rights and feelings, and you shouldn't really kill and eat it at all, or it's just carbon in a dynamic form?

Dave and I are comparing notes on the sports league this morning. My team is having a very victorious month, we are 12-3 up after the first two weeks of June. Dave needs to make some moves if he is to turn things round. He says he'll get the chess set and see me in the garden for a game after I have finished my breakfast. I have to reluctantly agree – a declined challenge is recorded as a loss – as he is much better at chess than me. So I will hobble out there in a minute or two.

Jock doesn't like being outside in the sun, it's too hot

for him, so he is going to stay indoors, but agrees to host a darts match after lunch if anyone is up for it. Sounds like a plan. We usually play darts in the evening, but my son is coming today and we are going to the pub.

I am really looking forward to him coming. I hope he is looking forward to it too. I remember when I used to go and visit my Dad. I don't think either of us enjoyed those visits.

***

"Sandpiper, it's your move," says Dave.

"Piper, are you asleep? Have you nodded off in the sun again? Just because I am near to checkmating you!"

He is right, I had nodded off, and he is about to win.

"That's alright," I say, tipping my king over. "I resign, now let me get back to my dreams. Wake me when it's time for lunch."

"Twelve four," says Dave and picks up the newspaper.

Election results are still being discussed on the front page.

"Why did you vote Labour?" asks Dave.

"Because I always have done so," I say

"OK, but why have you always done so? Doesn't it depend on what they stand for? Or whether they are likely to win?"

"Not really; that would be like picking the team you thought were going to win the premiership. You need to be loyal."

"But who you vote for makes a real difference to things. Supporting the winning team isn't the same."

"Who you vote for doesn't make any difference either, the chances of your vote deciding who runs the country are virtually zero."

"So why do you vote at all."

"Because."

"Because?"

"Because I believed in the Labour Party sixty years ago, and a better party hasn't come along since."

"Are you one of those people who would vote for a donkey if it stood as the Labour candidate?"

"I would explain to people how a donkey might be able to give us a fresh perspective on things."

***

Whatever the quality of my political thinking, I have always tried to act, or believe, in the right things.

I have been a member of the Labour Party ever since I was born. Technically not, I only joined at University, but it is definitely genetic in my family and, when I was growing up, probably compulsory in Wales. I joined all sorts of organisations when I got to University, but only political ones. This included the Anarchist Society, obviously a contradiction in terms. I studied Law and Politics, and the politics excited me.

I could passionately argue that there was no moral difference between abortion and early infanticide. I won a debate on the motion that sometimes you should give into terrorism. If someone threatens to kill a million people unless we give them an ice cream, is it really the right answer to allow the people to die? It is no use my opponents arguing that terrorists would never just ask for an ice cream, the principle is won. I am not sure I would want to make those points now, but at university sometimes you trivialised the extremely untrivial.

I read a lot of political thinking and could quote from much of it.

"Man is born free, but everywhere he is in chains."

"Social progress can be measured by the social position of the female sex."

212

"Every man has a property in his own person. This nobody has right to, but himself."

"An idea is always a generalisation, and generalisation is a property of thinking. To generalise means to think." (Does anyone understand Hegel?)

And my favourite of all, from John Stuart Mill.

"Not all conservatives are stupid people, but most stupid people are conservative."

I wrote, in the passionate vocabulary of a twenty-year old, about how equality was the only true freedom, and that the right to free speech was a middle-class luxury.

Then my stint at university ended and I had to get a job. Maybe I imagined that I would go into politics at some point, become a local councillor then an MP and then - who knows? I never did. I thought about it every so often, but it seems to me to be too much of a popularity contest, rather than finding the best candidates. I am still waiting for the people to recognise that talent in me and insist on me running the country but until then I remain a member of the Labour Party, did a few years as a governor at a Tottenham School and served for ten years as a vice-president of the Adele fan club.

"So, you are blindly loyal to Labour then?"

"I guess so," I said, "Yes. Although I resent the word 'blindly' because that implies that if I could see, I would see the error of my ways."

"The Labour Party believe in the things I believe in, that is why I vote for them."

"They founded the NHS, launched the living wage, introduced rent controls in London. They also introduced the Universal Basic Income and got rid of the House of Lords."

"...renewed Trident, helped take us out of the European Union."

"Yes, but those were things they needed to commit to, in order to get into power."

"So, there are no principles here, just power?"

"No, it's the other way round, the Labour party and I have principles. The Labour Party sometimes have to do things against their principles to be elected so as to deliver on their principles overall."

Joseph Sandpiper, a man of principles, with a sixty-year track record of voting Labour and paying my membership fees. I have not fallen into the stereotype of being left wing when I was young and then selling out as I get older and become part of the establishment. I was left wing when younger, liberal in my attitudes before most of my colleagues and peers, and, while I have become part of the establishment, I have not sold out and become right wing.

I still believe that the only way to really achieve change is for a group of "good men and women" with the right principles to lead and not allow themselves to be impeded by the democratic need to appeal to the people's perceived self-interest.

With the right insight and principles, that group could and should lead the changes that are needed to maximise human happiness. Maybe, once, I thought that such a group would actually emerge and that I would be part of them as a person who changed things. Now, sixty years later, I know I still believe that those things should change but also that a new generation will have to deliver it.

Over to Susie then.

***

It is nearly time for tea.

"Sandpiper. Joe, you said to wake you for tea."

Dave is tapping me on the knee.

"I'm awake."

"I was having a dream."

214

"What were you dreaming about?"

"My Mum."

"Is she still alive?"

"No, she'd be over a hundred by now. She died when she was 83."

"And your Dad?"

"My dad was younger than Mum, but he also died, about twenty years ago, he was 88."

"So, not bad ages then. And with all this miracle medicine they are giving us now, you'll last a long time"

"Hopefully," I say, "What's for lunch?"

"Fish and chips for us, you'll probably get another omelette."

"How was it being an architect?" I ask Dave

"It depended on the project. Sometimes there was a really great feeling from doing something new or working with a really creative client, but most of the time it was just haggling with engineers and local authorities over regulations and materials and traffic restrictions."

"What did you architect then?"

"All sorts of things. The Eltham bypass, two Tesco supermarkets, a new art gallery in Kent. Lots of private houses. Why do you ask?"

"Oh, just thinking about the job I had and what I got done."

"Didn't you win your clients lots of money?"

"Yes, but I didn't create anything. You built stuff."

"And Matilda taught lots of kids and wrote poems"

"Exactly, thanks for adding that!"

"Stop feeling sorry for yourself. You had a great career, you have kids and grandkids, what do you want, some sort of recognition?"

"No. I guess I never thought about it, I just did what came next, but I always thought I might create something. I was

215

in a band for ten minutes, I wrote poetry for twenty, I wrote kids stories for thirty..."

"Yes and you went to that painting class for an hour then quit!"

"Haha. Yes, I was always awful at art. I got 1% in my year four art exam. I drew two Wombles playing tennis. Lizzie was always quite good, and the kids are. We used to go to lots of galleries. I like art but I can't do it. I love music."

"So, create something now, write some music, write some more poems – I saw that one you one wrote for Matilda the other day, it wasn't bad. Take photos. Invent something. Build a sandcastle or grow some vegetables. Just don't try and define your life by that sort of thinking. Life is to be lived. Everyone contributes to the living of it."

"Fair enough", I say.

***

Someone is nudging me. It's Matilda.

"It's your move."

I look at the board, she has more pieces than me. I am going to lose, unless... no, I am going to lose.

"Who taught you to play chess?" I ask.

"My dad."

"What he was like?"

"I thought he was lovely when I was little but he treated my mum pretty badly later on, so I am not so sure. He loved me though, and was always good to me. Even when I got into trouble."

"You got into trouble?"

"Oh, loads of times. I was caught shoplifting, done for using a fake ID, arrested for a lie down protest during the Miners' Strike. I have been arrested three times. I spent a night in the jail after the Miners thing."

And she writes poetry, how cool is Matilda?

"You?"

"I have never been arrested but I was nearly twice."

"For what?"

"For arson."

"Really?"

"Well, sort of arson."

Helen comes over.

"I've just had a call from Ian. He's running late but he will still pop in, he should be here by ten."

"Thanks. In that case I am a bit tired, I think I'll go to my room."

"Aren't you going to finish the game?" asked Matilda.

My king falls on its side.

"You were going to win."

"Are you going to bed too?"

"No. I'll send Ian in when he gets here. I'll see you after he's gone. Don't fall asleep. He's making the effort to come and see you."

"Yes, but I have made the effort to stay up, and now he's late."

"Poor you."

I do fall asleep.

Ian wakes me.

"Hey dad."

"Sorry I'm late, I had a last-minute meeting at work. So by the time I got on the motorway it was eight o clock."

"Eight? So, you must have driven ridiculously fast."

"Yes, probably, but I made it, not before you've gone to bed though, I see."

I sit up in bed, we hug, and Ian kisses me on the forehead. It is really good to see him.

"I saw Matilda on my way in. She says she would have come to the pub with us, but it is a bit late now."

"Next time," I say. "How's Mum?"

"She's great, she sends her best. Says you and Matilda should come down to London soon."

"How are Ling and the kids?"

"Great too."

"And you?"

"Ok, what about you?"

"A bit tired but OK. You must be tired, working all day and then driving all that way? Where are you staying?

"They have guest rooms here, so I'll use one of them."

"So we can have breakfast together?"

"Yes sure, assuming you get up! I said to Ling that I would be back by oneish so we should have time."

"Great."

"How's work?"

"Busy."

"Good busy?"

"Yes, sure, busy mean we make money."

"Lots, Mum tells me!"

"We do OK. Although there's more to life than money Dad."

"Yeah, but you enjoy what you do also."

"Sometimes. Sometimes there's a great new client or a great team or a tough problem to solve. But much of it is the same. Once you have done two dozen growth strategy projects, how much new can there be?"

"Maybe you need to change firms, you've been there a while."

"The firm's great, so is the job. I just wonder what else is out there. I still wonder about whether we should have gone to China before we had the kids. Now they are in the UK schooling systems it would be so much tougher to move them, but that sticks us here for another ten years at least. I'll be 50."

It isn't like Ian to sound sorry for himself, he is always

upbeat and having a great time.

"Do you wish had done different things with your life, Dad?"

"No, other than still being with your Mum, no. I have had a much better, and longer, life than I expected. And once you have children, you need to think about what's best for them too. Mum would have maybe let me do different things otherwise, but she was very strong that our first duty was to you and Susie."

"I feel the same about Zack and Annie, as does Ling, they come first. But there are lots of non-reckless alternate ways to live your life. I feel sometimes that we should try a few."

I am not going to say this to Ian - Lizzie will not forgive me if I do - but he is right. He's never said he feels like this before, and maybe he hasn't, but I feel like this all the time.

Not just about big things, about little ones, or silly ones too. I smoked for too, too long. I never did anything with my strongly held political beliefs, I never wrote my book, and I wish I'd slept with more women than I have. I don't regret my career, or having the kids, or all that time with Lizzie. I wish I had spent more time with my Mum and Dad, and Laura. Maybe I shouldn't have stayed at one firm for my whole career. Why did I have to wait until I was old to go back to Wales? How many proper friends had I ever had? How much money had I wasted on therapists and health checks?

"My test." I say, "is whether I ever meet people whose lives I envied, whose life I thought was better than mine. There weren't many. And even for those few, I could always find a reason why I couldn't be them."

"I don't want to be someone else. I just want to do something else."

"Isn't it the same thing?"

"How do you mean?"

"I think you do the things you are, or are the things you do. One of those ways round. I'm a single Welsh ex lawyer grandparent. You're an English (Welsh really but you won't accept it) consultant, husband and father."

"Isn't it how you are, not just what – are you successful, happy, kind, fulfilled, nurturing – all those questions. What sort of man you are?"

"Ah, now that's tougher. I was a good lawyer, a good father, an OK husband, and OK son, an intermittent grandad, a rubbish poet."

"I think you've been, and are, great. You're my dad so I am not going to judge you too harshly, but I would be happy to have lived my life as you lived yours. I hope Ling and I stay together – we will – but I would also like to try some other stuff, to travel some other paths."

"Ling's brother has been in touch to ask whether I she and I want to move to Guangdong and run the family company. I am going to say yes. I have spoken to Mum, she understands. She will miss the kids, but she'll have to come to China. As will you."

I hardly ever see Zack and Annie as it is. Ian knows that. Guangdong (wherever that is) is a long way from London, even further from the Gower.

'When are you going?"

"September, probably."

"Wow, not long."

"No."

"Sounds great."

"Let's talk tomorrow morning about getting you down to London before we go."

"Sounds good."

"Can I get you anything before you then? A cup of tea maybe?"

'Tea would be good, and a cigarette!"

"Funny. I'll get the tea. I'll be back in a minute Dad."

***

Ian comes back. No cup of tea in hand.

"Where's my tea?"

"No tea. Come on, we're going for a walk."

"But it's late, I'm in my bed, and it's dark outside."

"Life is here to be lived, Dad, come on. Don't worry about getting dressed, let's put your coat on and you can go out in your pyjamas and slippers! Don't worry about your knee, I'll borrow someone's wheelchair."

So I find myself, night garbed, being wheeled past reception. No one seems to notice. I guess it is unlikely that someone would abduct their own father, although we aren't supposed to be out of the house after 9 o'clock.

It is dark outside but not too cold. Quiet though, I can already hear the waves. I can see flames on the beach, and figures, and hear voices. Someone is having a beach bonfire.

Ian wheels me to the top of the steps down to the beach. Are we going down there, how is he going to get me down those? There are people, shadows, coming up the steps.

"Hi Dad," says Susie. She is there with Jake and someone I do not recognise. Between the four of them they simply lift me and my chair and carry me down the steps.

And towards the bonfire. "Hey, Susie, I wasn't expecting you here."

"I'm here for the party, we all are."

"Whose party? What are we celebrating?"

"Life."

"Sounds great. Who's here?"

"Everyone."

"Is Mum here?"

"Yes."

"Where?"

"Over there, playing with Zack and Annie."

There she is – Lizzie – I haven't seen her for ages. She looks beautiful. If I didn't know better I would assume that Zack and Annie were her children not the generation after–she looks so happy and so young.

It makes me feel old, and sad. Ian asks me why I am crying.

"I'm just so happy to see you all –the family back together."

"Just for tonight, Dad, then we will all have to say goodbye."

"Sure, I understand. You are off to China, but this is wonderful."

There are lots of other people around the fire too. Who are they?

Someone bounds up to me. It is Andy. Andy Pritchard. "Hey Sandy, how are you doing? Where have you been all my life?"

"Here and there. You?"

"Here, I stayed in Wales. Jo and I got married, even though you stole her virginity!"

"I think it was the other way round!

"Is that Peter and William over there? It looks like them sat near the fire."

"Yes, William's mum said they could come, so long as we don't get Peter run over this time!"

"Good to see you."

"And you guys" – what is going on?

It is Dev and his wife. "I see your dress sense hasn't improved, you're here in your pyjamas and slippers. At least the coat is new!"

Dev has come with the rest of them, Stuart, Kev and David. And out of the corner of my eye I spot Dawn talking to

Lizzie. That might not go so well.

Cosmopolitan appears.

"What shall we sing?" asks Dave, as he picks up his guitar.

"Let's do that hippy one that Robin hates."

Robin laughs.

"Let's see if you can get the drum bit right this time!"

I pick up my drumsticks –where have they come from - and riff on the high hat.

A small crowd has formed. I recognise some of them but not all – Lizzie is there with Andy, Eric and Lesley, Jane and John Andrew – so that lasted too!

I think I see Ian Curtis in the crowd, and Siouxsie Sioux, Adele and Phil Lynott, but I must be imagining things. Next will be Tony Blair and Troy Deeney – hold on, no it's just the firelight, playing with my eyes.

"One, two, three four," and off we go.

Everyone joins Robin in the chorus.

"Here's to the happiest of days
Here's to our best of friends
Here's to the planet earth
Here's to lives without ends"

I know, hippy or what. Robin has always said he hated it but this time he sang it with a Morrissey like world weariness.

We play all of our Cosmopolitan classics, we do an awesome version of Calon Lan, everyone joins in and Laura plays violin over our rhythm section. We play The Boys are Back in Town as an encore, and Phil joins us on "stage". It is awesome, we are awesome, and the crowd love it.

I am crying again. Ian smiles.

"I love you dad."

"I love you too son. I always will"

Then I see them. Some things are so sad that you can't cry. My Mum and Dad are there. They are sat together by the fire, holding hands. I don't have the heart to interrupt them, so I just watch for a bit.

When I was a child, I thought my parents would live forever. I worried about my dying, but it never, really, as a child, occurred to me that people I loved, who loved me, would die too. Now my parents have gone and, if I think about it too hard, I realise that the same will happen to me and Lizzie and, one day, our children.

That's just not acceptable, is it?

Susie and Jake come over to sit with me. Angel is with them.

Susie smiles, that heart-warming smile of hers. "We've got some news," she said, grasping Jake's hand with her left and pointing to her stomach with her right.

"We're having another little one, at last."

"Oh wow that's so great. Is it Jake's?" I asked, inappropriate humour again, and smile back.

She sits on my lap and put my hand on her stomach. "If it's a boy we're going to name it Joseph. If it's a girl then Catherine."

"When is it due?"

"September."

"I can't wait to introduce it to Elvis and Presley!"

"I can't wait for you to do that too."

"Mum must be pleased, a new baby in the family."

"Give her my love."

"You should tell her."

"I will."

"And I love you and Jake and the little one, it's so amazing."

Another group approaches, led by Matilda.

"Did you hear that? Susie and Jake are having a baby."

What is Matilda doing on the beach at this time of night? Why is she dressed like a princess? She has on one of those Disney princesses costumes that Susie had loved so much when she was little. Belle, maybe, from Beauty and the Beast, or is it Cinderella? And there are Jock and Dave, dressed as pirates. This beach bonfire is becoming surreal.

"Ooh Arr, Dave lad," I say.

"We've come to take you back to your bed" says Matilda. "It's late and it's too cold out here, you'll catch your death."

"Yes, but all my family and friends are here."

"We're your friends and family now."

"We've even dressed up to entertain you." – they know I love Disneyworld. Every time I am asked for my best holiday, I trot out our Florida trip when the kids had been ten and twelve.

"I don't want to go back. I want to stay on this beach forever."

"Well, I'm not staying with you, Joseph. You know your family don't like me."

"They do, you think they somehow see you as a reason why Lizzie and I haven't got back together but they are wrong, and I've told them. Lizzie doesn't want me back."

"But you would go back if she wanted you."

"Yes, I guess I would, but I have loved being with you too."

Lizzie comes over. "Can I borrow him Matilda?"

"Of course. Bye Joe."

"Come on," says Lizzie, and grabs the handles of my chair. She pushes me away from the fire and towards the sea.

We are alone.

"Can you stand?"

"I can give it go. It's only my knee. I hurt it playing

225

cricket."

My knee does not protest. It knows it has to make the effort. I stand next to her. Despite the wind, she manages to light two cigarettes and hand me one.

"These are bad for us," I say

"I know, but it's just one."

"Are you happy to see everyone?"

"I am happy to see you most of all."

"And me you."

We stand and smoke them slowly. I watch my friends and family dance. Backgrounded by a haze of fire, moonlight and cigarette smoke, is this what it was like being on drugs? I really must try them.

"Let's sit on the beach, leave your chair there."

She helps me sit.

I can feel the sand under my clothes. I take my slippers off and wiggle my toes in it.

"Isn't the tide coming in?" I ask.

"Yes," she says, "but let's not worry about that," puts her arms through mine and holds me close. Lizzie kisses me.

Laura comes over and sits down next to us.

"What are you doing?"

"We're waiting for the tide to come in."

At the seaside (written in 1978)

The copper rays
Of the dying sun
Silhouette the wretched body
Swaying in the last whispers
Of the wind
And waves

He rose

226

To the crash of breakers
On the weed strewn rocks
Turned
Slowly
To the howl of the wind
And the thundering waves

Death bore
No horror for him now
Moving silently
From sand to sea
Leaving footprints
An epitaph to a man
Whipped by the wind
Drowned by the waves

Ian comes back into the room with a cup of tea.

"Dad, I've got your tea."

"Dad."

He touches me on the cheek. I am cold.

He presses the intercom. Helen answers.

"Helen, Helen, I can't wake him!"

The water is cold now and I can only breathe by standing on tiptoes. The moonlight lets me see far out to sea. I turn back to the beach. The fire has gone out and my friends have gone home. I feel like I have a decision to make. I can let the waves take me. Or I can fight. Do something!

I have no memory of what happened after that. There is no me to do the remembering.

15 December 2020

Thanks for reading my book

When I started writing this - as a middle-aged man – it was going to be about how tough men's lives are, informed by how tough I thought mine was.

I do think life can be tough and that my experience of the challenges will be a man's one. When I said this to a male friend, he responded with,

"I agree, we need an 'us too' movement."

I am not sure he quite got the point, but maybe some of what I meant to say is his story too. I finished the first draft of these words while waiting for my wife to return from the inaugural conference of the Women's Equality Party. I don't, for a nanosecond, think that there is no justification for a positive push to redress inequality even if the consequence is a real or perceived negative impact on the rest of us. For every gender inequality, add in multiples of that for race and for the disadvantaged in every society. These things are not sustainable, nor would it be acceptable to try and sustain and defend them.

That's what progress requires, and I think the push to drive acceptance and equality amongst all groups is hugely important. I am, in that regard, a whining liberal. I am also struck by the recent increase in recognition of mental health issues and also the appallingly sad outing of years of child abuse.

But there have also been backward steps. As the material quality of life has improved in the developed world (although clearly not anything like equally enough, never mind the rest of the world) so the emotional and spiritual qualities of life have, in my view, deteriorated.

Most of believe or know we are here for a finite time.

Many of us will live for years beyond what our ancestors dreamed of but without the physical or financial or emotional wherewithal to make the most of it. Many families live physically and emotionally separate lives.

I am trying to reconcile the high quality of life I see available to many with the levels of stress, friction and pain, which I see and hear in those people. Maybe I am at the half empty end of the spectrum, maybe everyone else is happy all the time, maybe most men don't think about death every day.

I expected those things to feature in what I wrote, and I hope they do. But a couple of more things came out too, and they surprised me.

There are a lot more 'happy memories' (Let's remember this is fiction, not an autobiography) in this book than I expected.

And for a book by a grumpy middle age man there are two quite strong love stories in this book. Again, that was not what I expected.

One is quite clear – whoever Lizzie is, she is clearly at the centre of my world.

The other is less clear, although he is also central. It's an attempt to love myself. I will keep trying to do that while resting on the hearts of those who love me. They know who they are, and I wanted to thank them for giving me the strength and time to put some of this down on paper. I love them too.

Rhys

Printed in Great Britain
by Amazon

29276731R00129